·THE· HISTRONAUTS
A VIKING ADVENTURE

Written by
FRANCES DURKIN

Illustrated by
GRACE COOKE

Designed by
VICKY BARKER

JOLLY
FiSH
PRESS

Text © Frances Durkin 2018
Illustrations © Grace Cooke 2018

Book design by Vicky Barker
Illustrations by Grace Cooke

First published in the United Kingdom by b small publishing ltd.

Published in the United States by Jolly Fish Press, an imprint of North Star Editions, Inc.

First US Edition
First US Printing, 2019

This is a work of fiction. Names, characters, places, and incidents are either the product of the author's imagination or are used fictitiously, and any resemblance to actual persons living or dead, business establishments, events, or locales is entirely coincidental.

Library of Congress Cataloging-in-Publication Data
Names: Durkin, Frances, 1981- author. | Cooke, Grace, illustrator.
Title: A Viking adventure / by Frances Durkin ; illustrated by Grace Cooke.
Description: Mendota Heights, MN : Published in the United States
    by Jolly Fish Press, an imprint of North Star Editions, Inc., 2020. |
    Series: The Histronauts | Originally published in the United Kingdom
    by b small publishing in 2018. | Summary: The Histronauts travel
    back in time to the Viking era to forage for food, decipher runes,
    build beautiful burial boats, and learn all about a Viking raid.
Identifiers: LCCN 2019014330 (print) | LCCN 2019019207 (ebook) | ISBN
    9781631633652 (ebook) | ISBN 9781631633645 (pbk.) | ISBN
    9781631633638 (hardcover)
Subjects: | CYAC: Vikings–Fiction. | Time travel–Fiction. | LCGFT:
    Historical fiction.
Classification: LCC PZ7.1.D87 Vi 2019 (ebook) | LCC PZ7.1.D87 Vi 2019 (print) | DDC
    [Fic]–dc23
LC record available at https://lccn.loc.gov/2019014330

Jolly Fish Press
North Star Editions, Inc.
2297 Waters Drive
Mendota Heights, MN 55120
www.jollyfishpress.com

Printed in the United States of America

Contents

Meet

The Histronauts

Luna

Age: Eight years
Likes: History, adventures, animals, problem solving, and storytelling
Dislikes: Getting lost and bad smells
Favorite Color: Blue
Favorite Food: Beans on toast
Favorite Place: Castles

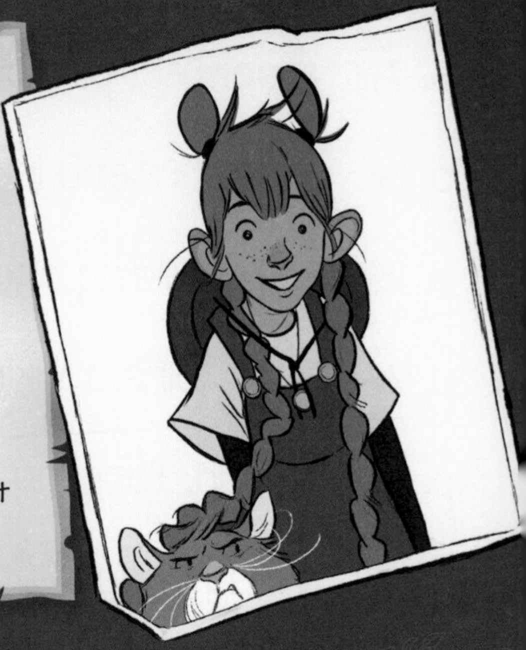

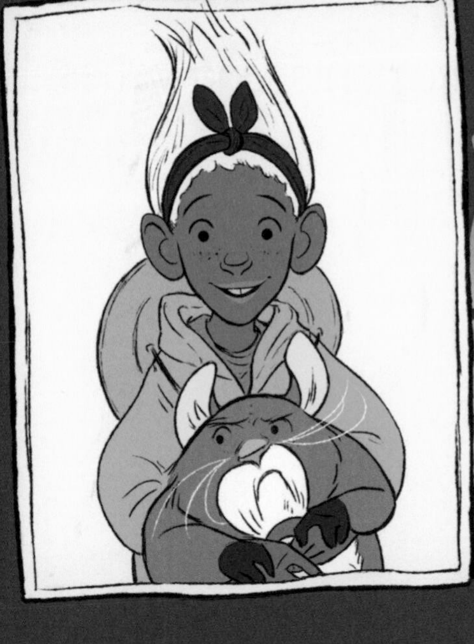

Nani

Age: Seven and a half years
Likes: Science, nature, math, gardening, flowers, and exploring
Dislikes: People who don't recycle
Favorite Color: Green
Favorite Food: Anything green
Favorite Place: Anywhere outside but mostly forests

Newton

Age: Ten years
Likes: Making things, eating, reading, cooking, and playing games
Dislikes: Being hungry and being cold
Favorite Color: Yellow
Favorite Food: Everything!
Favorite Place: Home

Hero

Age: Five years
Likes: Sleeping, being Luna's cat
Dislikes: Getting wet
Favorite Food: Chicken
Favorite Place: Curled up on the sofa

Timeline

The Viking Age began when Norse people from modern-day Sweden, Norway, and Denmark left their homelands to settle in new places.

AD 793
The first Viking raids on Lindisfarne in northern England take place.

AD 799
The Vikings raid the Aquitaine region in France.

AD 810
The first Viking raids in Frisia (now Holland) take place.

AD 839
The Vikings found the city of Dublin.

AD 860
Vikings attack Constantinople.

AD 867
The city of York is captured by the Vikings.

AD 874
The first Vikings settle in Iceland.

AD 911
King Charles III of France gives Normandy to the Vikings.

AD 980S
The Vikings adapt to Christianity when they take over Christian lands.

AD 982
Erik the Red discovers Greenland.

AD 1000
Leif Eriksson arrives in North America.

AD 1066
Norwegian King Harald Hardrada tries to invade England but is killed by English King Harold Godwinson.

AD 1100
There are no more Viking voyages and the Viking Age ends.

Numismatics

- Numismatics is the study and collection of money, such as coins and banknotes.
- People who study numismatics are called numismatists.
- Numismatists can use currency such as coins to tell us who was making and spending money.
- We know a lot about where the Vikings traded and who they traded with from the discovery and study of coins.

A perfect picnic

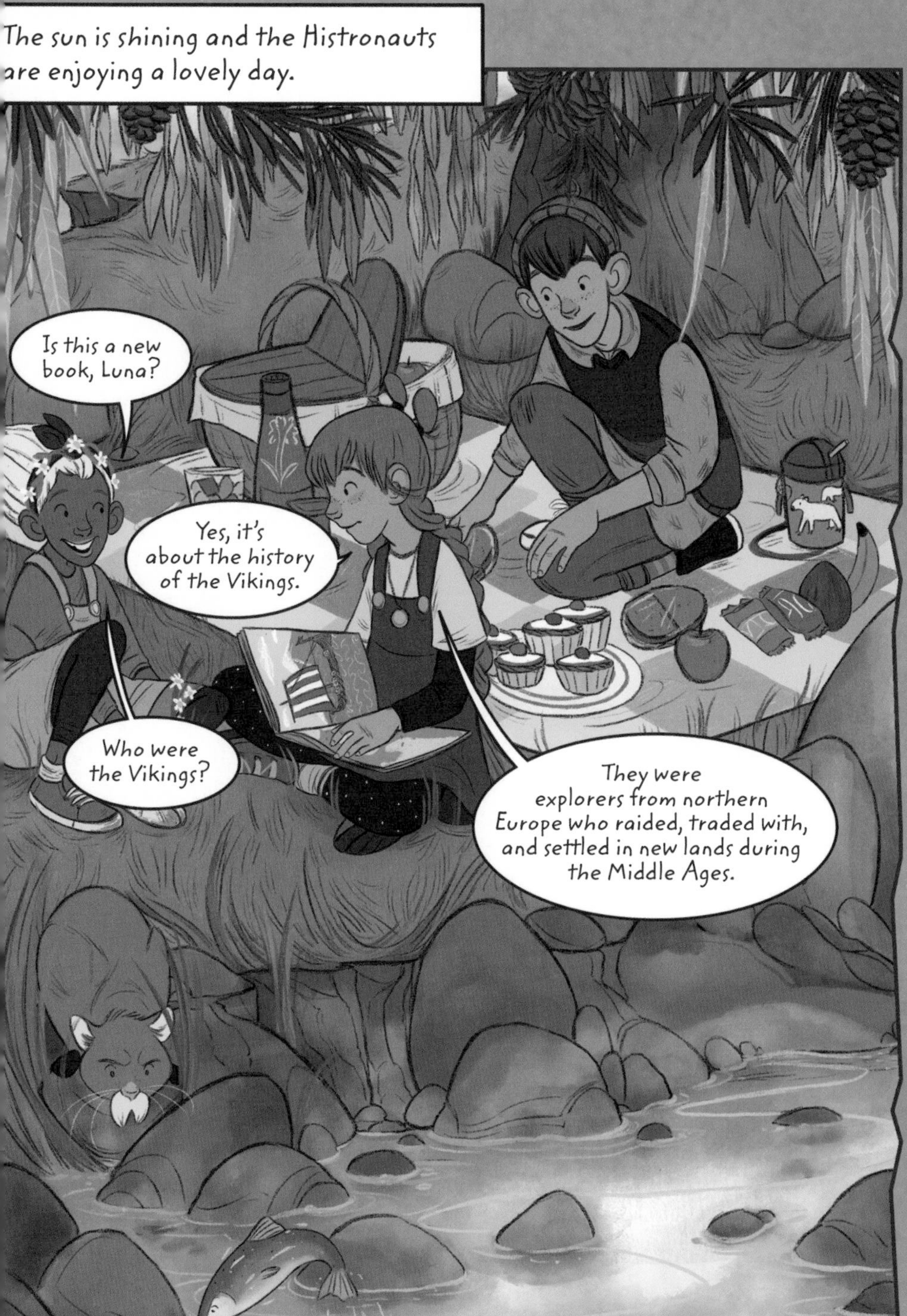

The sun is shining and the Histronauts are enjoying a lovely day.
Is this a new book, Luna?
Yes, it's about the history of the Vikings.
Who were the Vikings?
They were explorers from northern Europe who raided, traded with, and settled in new lands during the Middle Ages.

Map of Viking lands

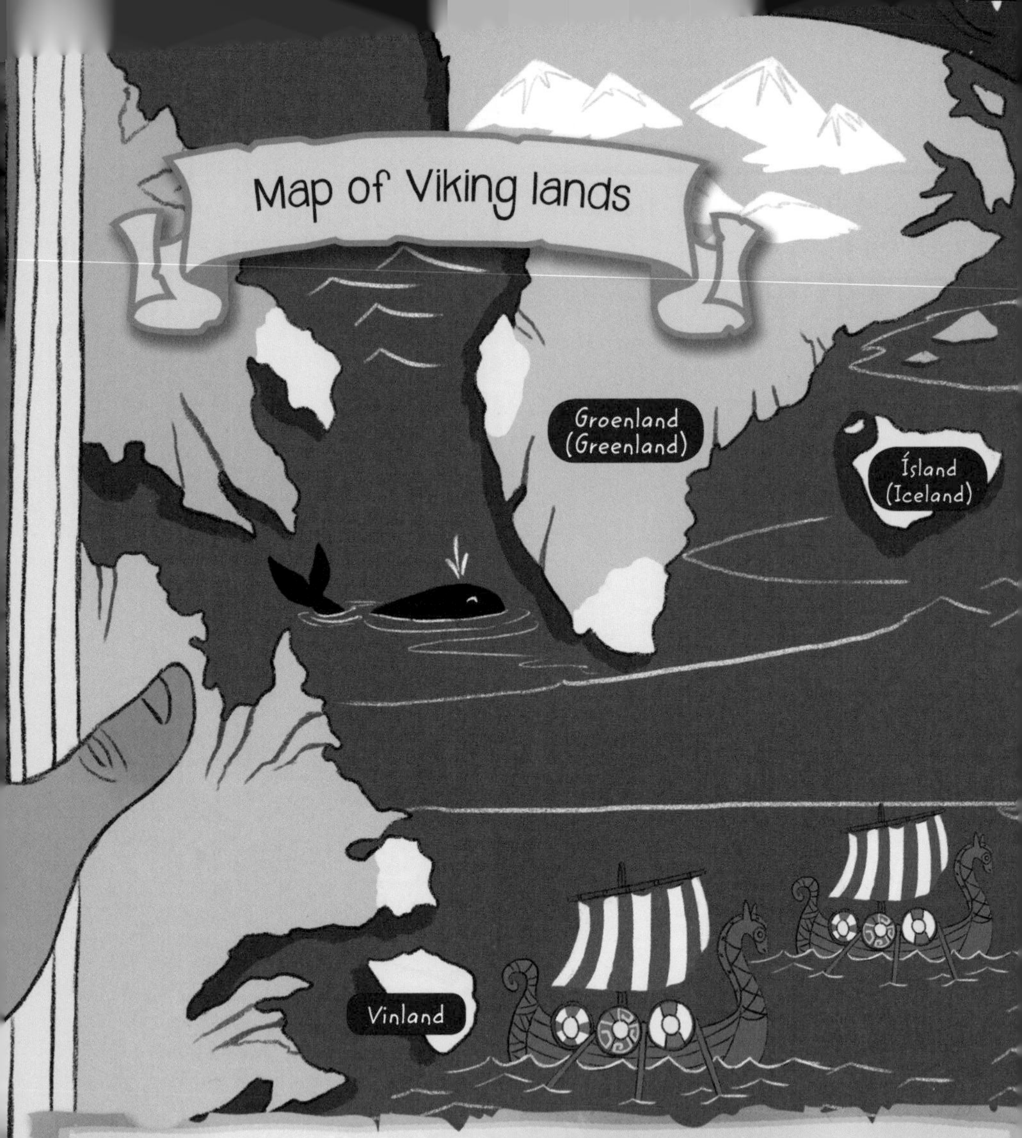
Groenland
(Greenland)
Ísland
(Iceland)
Vinland

The Vikings used descriptive words to name the places that they settled. Some places still have clues to their Viking origins. Do you live in a place with a Viking name?

- In Old Norse, the word *by* meant farm or village. Hedeby in Germany and Whitby in England were once Viking villages.
- A woodland clearing was called a *thveit*. Bracquetuit in France still has a hint of this name.
- Thorpe in Yorkshire gets its name from the Old Norse word *torp*, which meant small settlement.
- *Toft* meant homestead. Toftir in the Faroe Islands takes its name from this word.

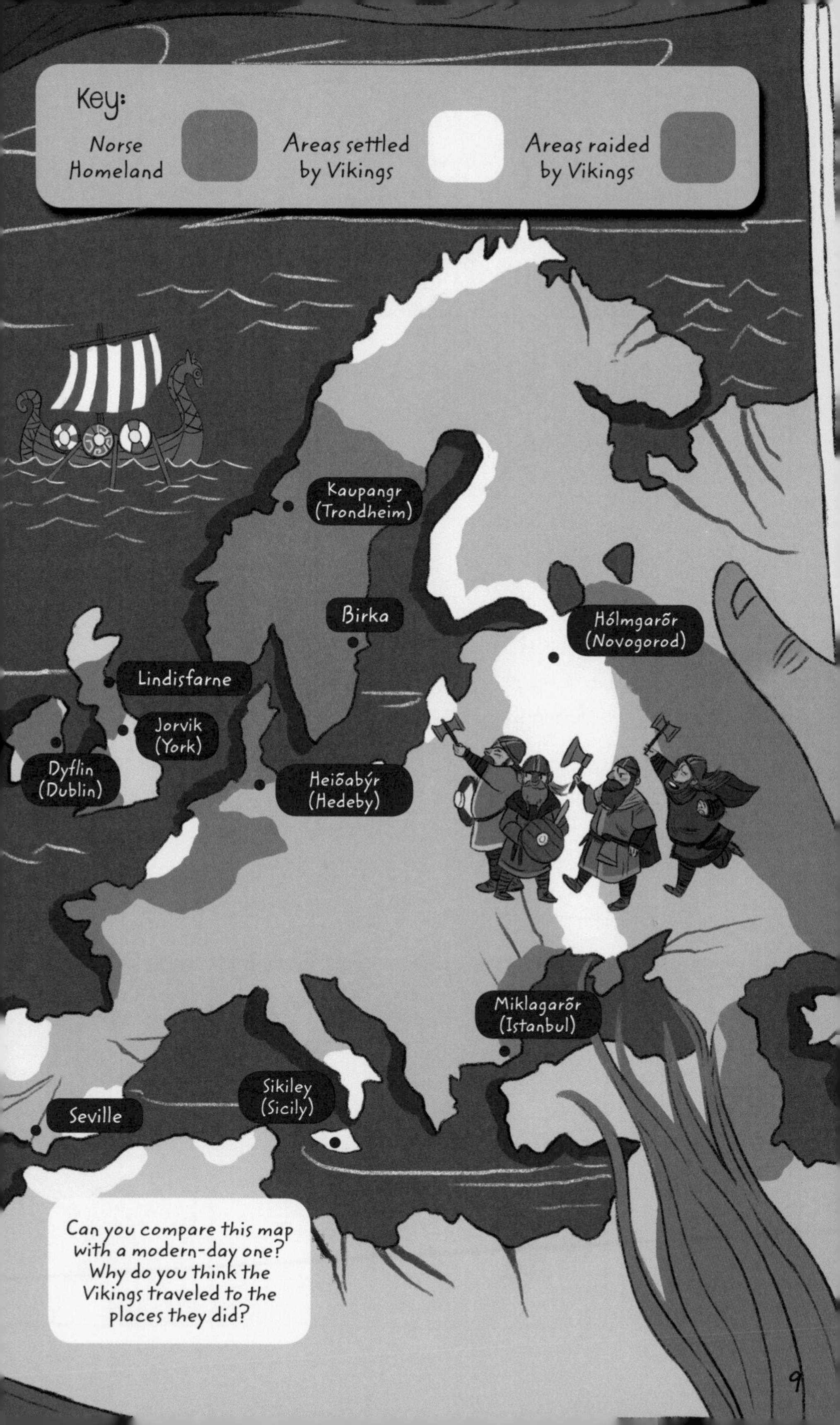
Key:
Norse Homeland
Areas settled by Vikings
Areas raided by Vikings
Kaupangr (Trondheim)
Birka
Hólmgarðr (Novogorod)
Lindisfarne
Jorvik (York)
Dyflin (Dublin)
Heiðabýr (Hedeby)
Miklagarðr (Istanbul)
Sikiley (Sicily)
Seville
Can you compare this map with a modern-day one? Why do you think the Vikings traveled to the places they did?

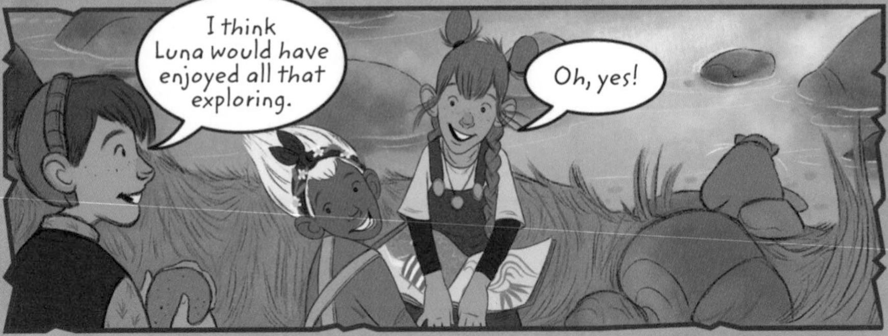
I think Luna would have enjoyed all that exploring.
Oh, yes!

Essential Viking Facts

The word *Viking* comes from a language that we call *Old Norse*.

A *vikingr* was a Norse person who went on an expedition to seek their fortune.

Vikings came from the countries in northern Europe that we now call Sweden, Norway, and Denmark.

It was usually in summer when they left their homes and sailed out to discover new places.

The Vikings settled in places as far apart as North America, England, and Russia.

They sold and traded goods such as furs, wool, wood, fish, and leather all over Europe and even as far away as Central Asia.

Vikings also brought unusual ingredients and objects such as spices, silks, and precious metals back to their homelands from around the world.

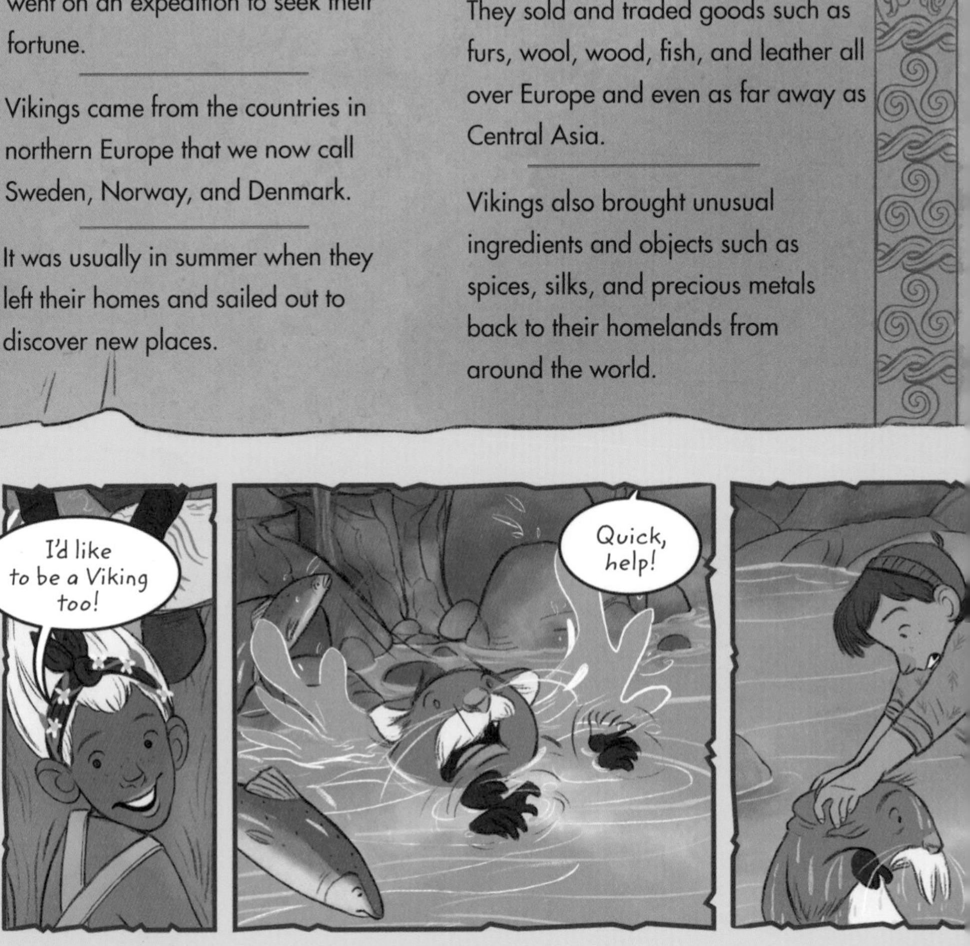
I'd like to be a Viking too!
Quick, help!

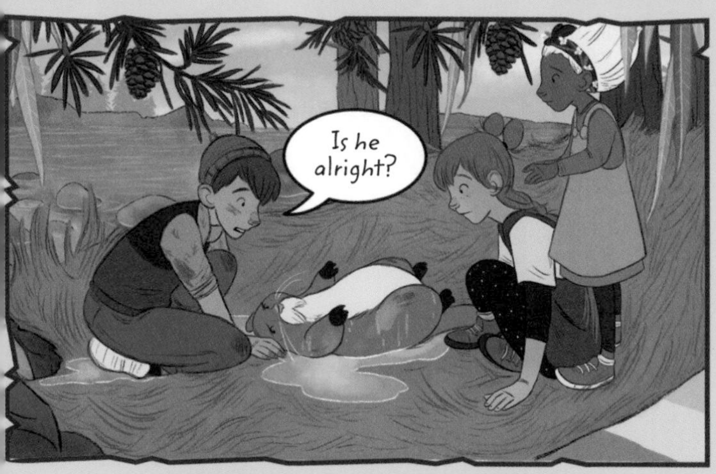
Is he alright?

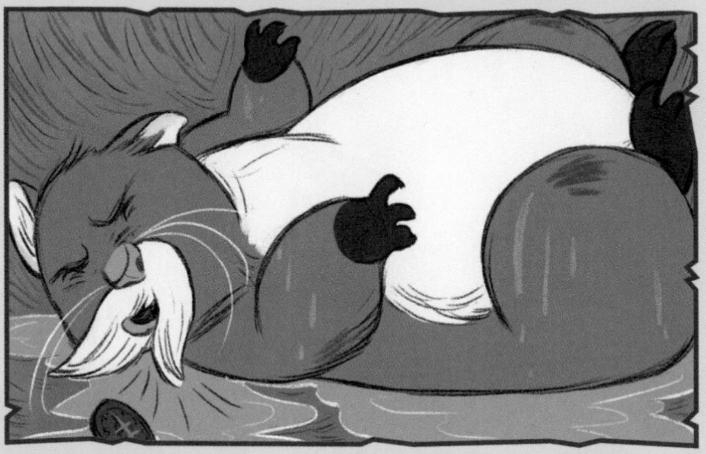

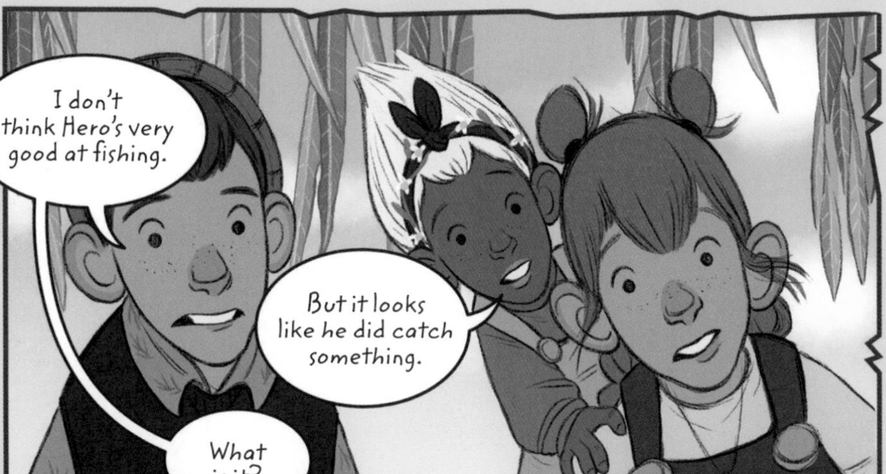
I don't think Hero's very good at fishing.
What is it?
But it looks like he did catch something.

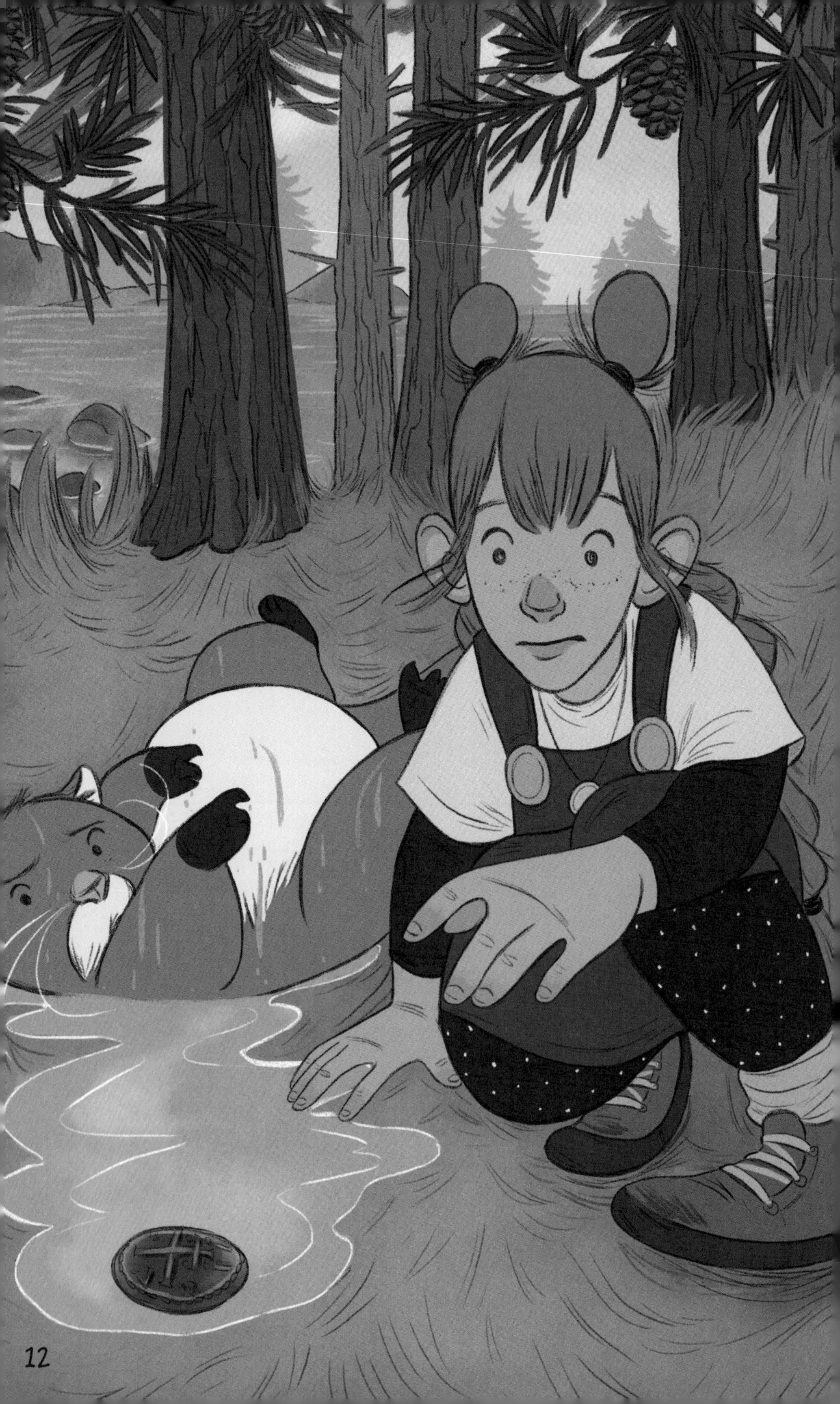

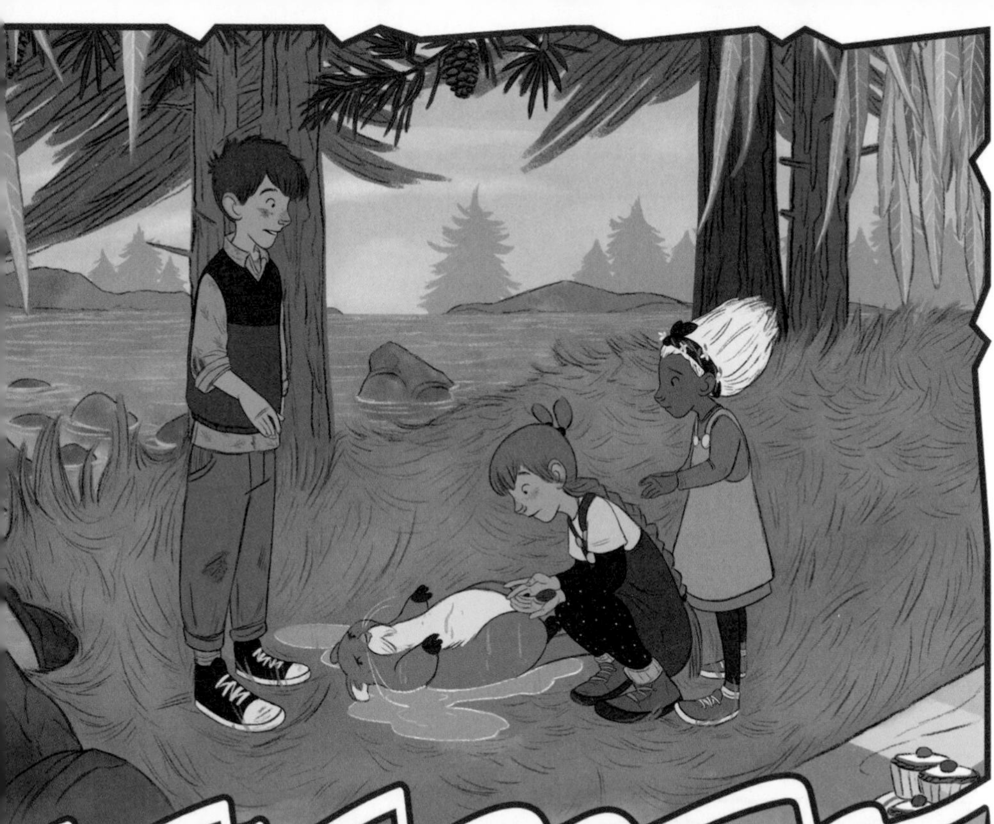

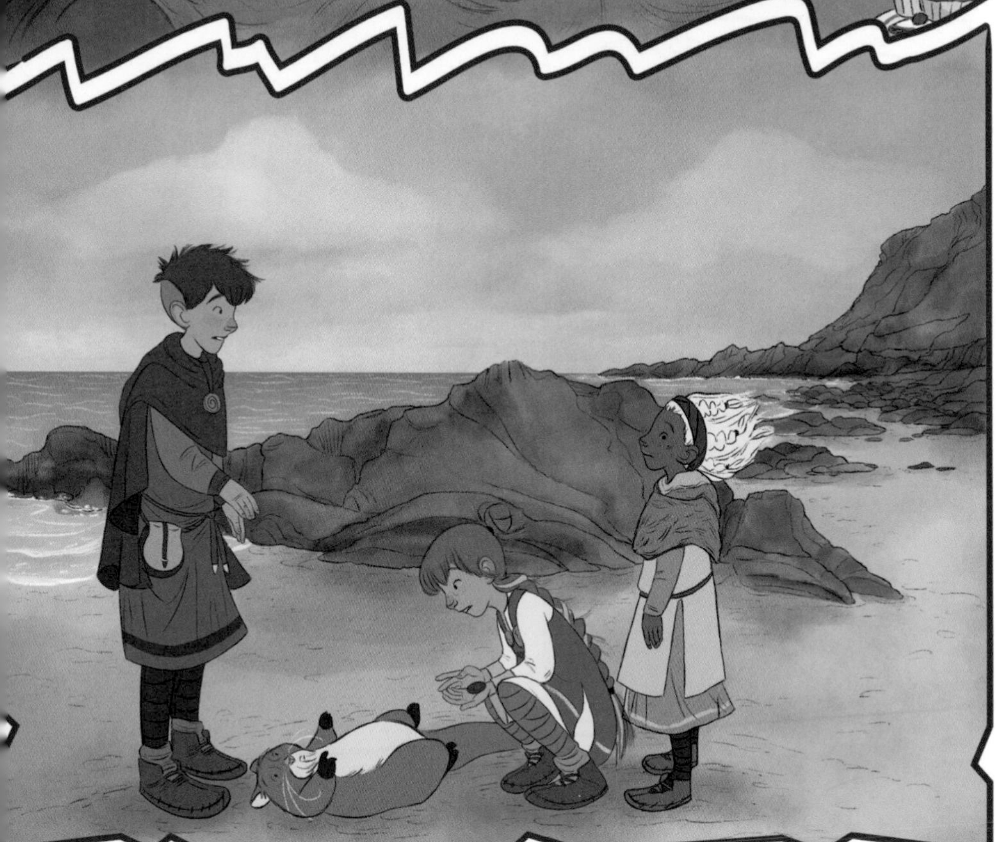

A new friend in the fjords

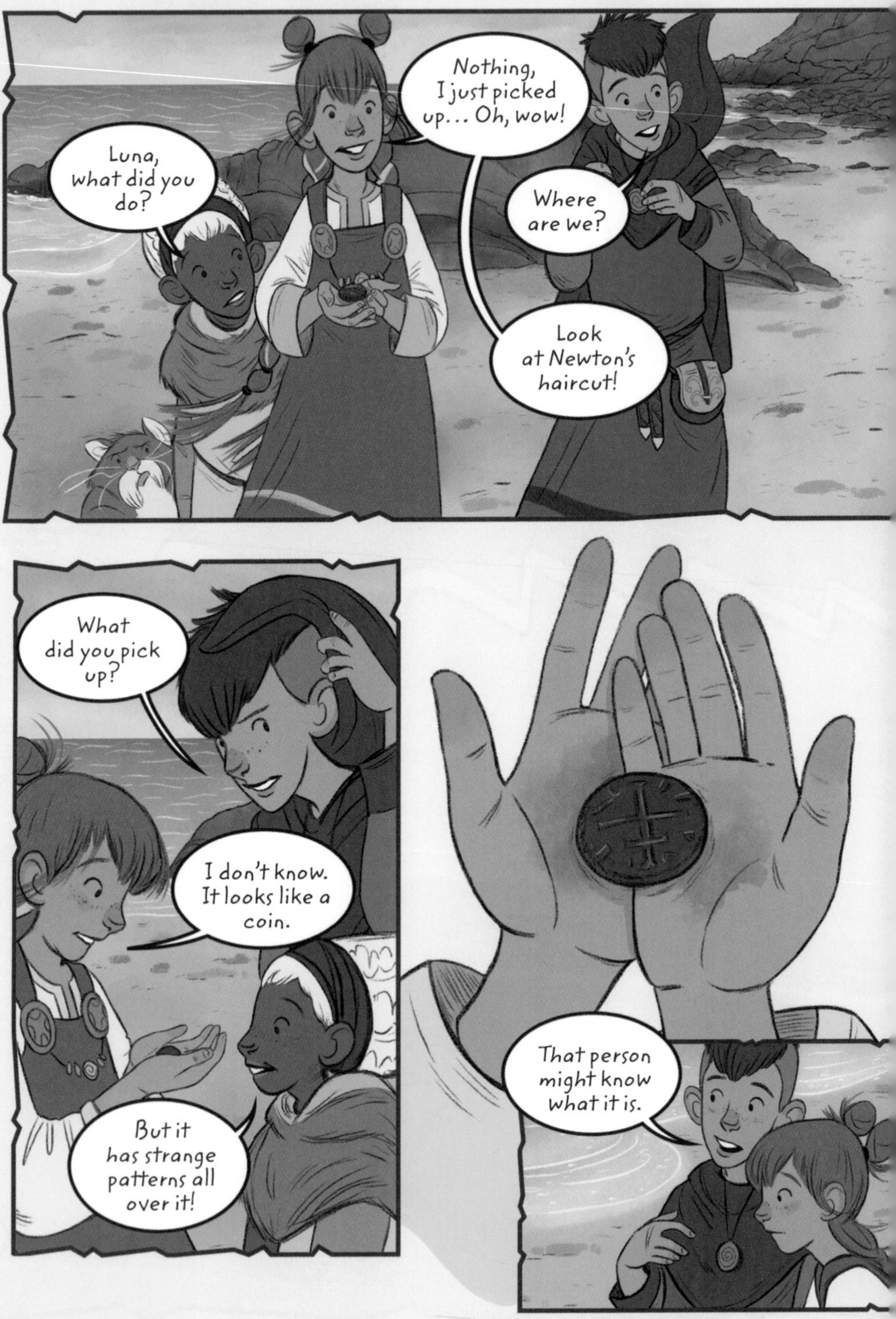
Luna, what did you do?
Nothing, I just picked up… Oh, wow!
Where are we?
Look at Newton's haircut!
What did you pick up?
I don't know. It looks like a coin.
But it has strange patterns all over it!
That person might know what it is.

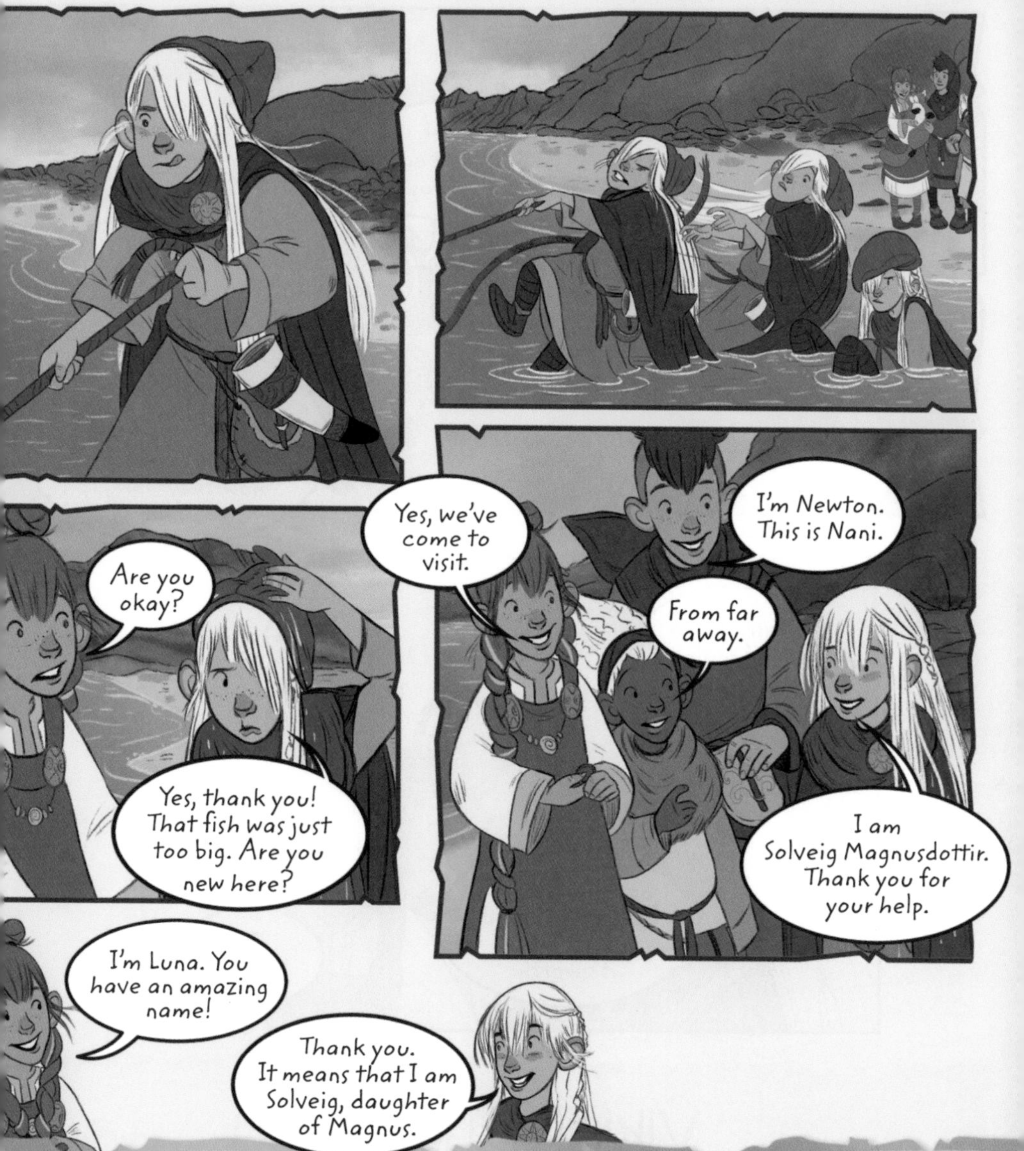
Are you okay?
Yes, thank you! That fish was just too big. Are you new here?
Yes, we've come to visit.
I'm Newton. This is Nani.
From far away.
I am Solveig Magnusdottir. Thank you for your help.
I'm Luna. You have an amazing name!
Thank you. It means that I am Solveig, daughter of Magnus.

Viking names

- Viking surnames are made by adding the name of the father to the word *son* or *dottir* (which means daughter).
- This type of name is called a *patronymic*.
- Solveig's brother's name is Bjorn Magnusson, which means that he is Bjorn, son of Magnus.
- Their father is called Magnus Eriksson, which means that he is Magnus, son of Erik.

Can you work out what your Viking name is?

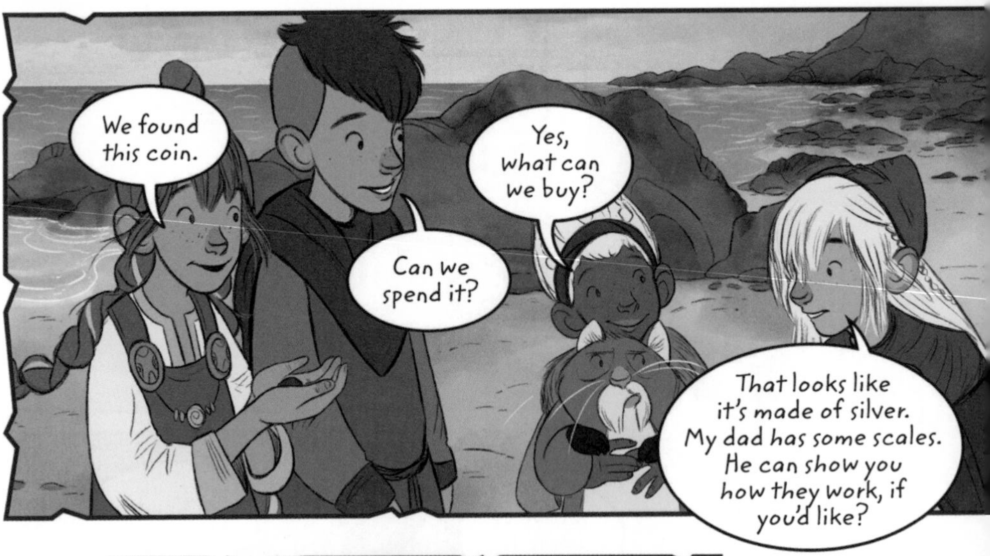
We found this coin.
Can we spend it?
Yes, what can we buy?
That looks like it's made of silver. My dad has some scales. He can show you how they work, if you'd like?

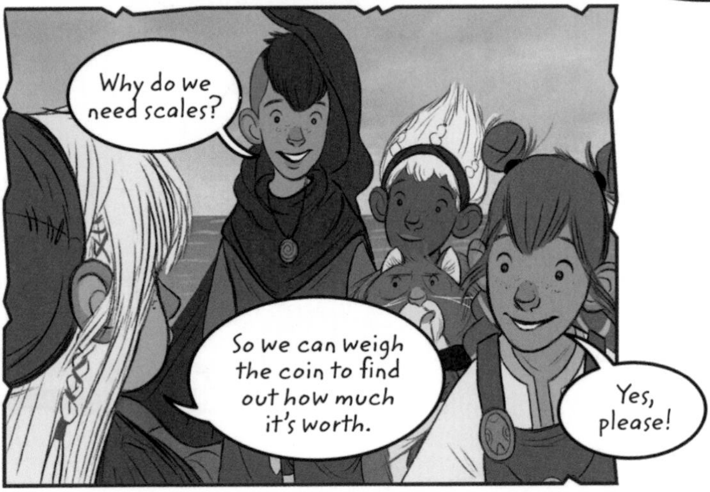
Why do we need scales?
So we can weigh the coin to find out how much it's worth.
Yes, please!

Viking currency

- When they first began to explore the world, the Vikings did not use coins.
- They traded with valuable objects instead, such as furs or pieces of precious metal such as silver.
- These pieces of silver were either lumps called *ingots* or broken pieces of jewelry called *hacksilver*.
- As they raided and traded with more cultures, the Vikings received coins.
- These coins had a set weight, which meant that their value always stayed the same.

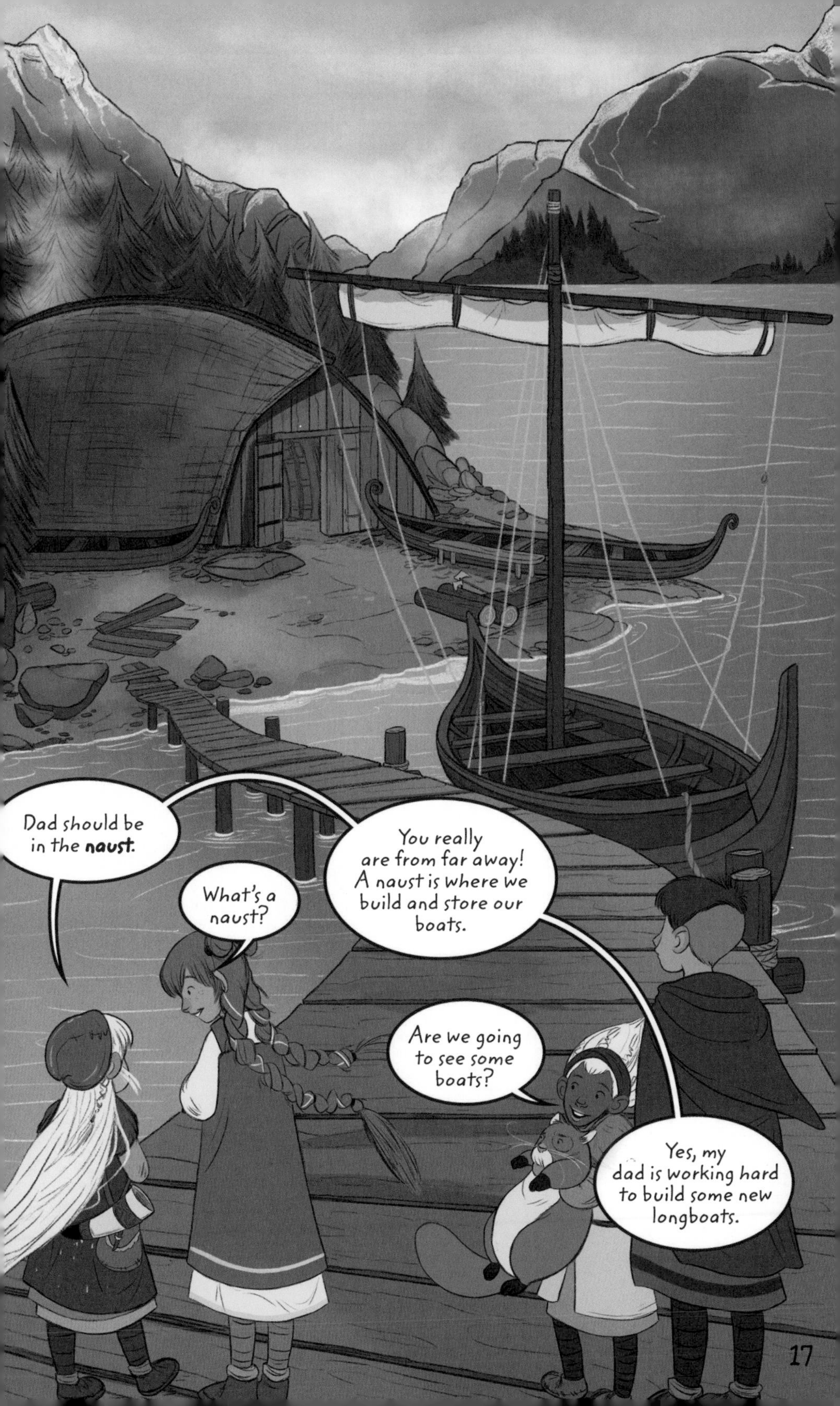
Dad should be in the **naust**.
What's a naust?
You really are from far away! A naust is where we build and store our boats.
Are we going to see some boats?
Yes, my dad is working hard to build some new longboats.

Boat building and nautical navigation

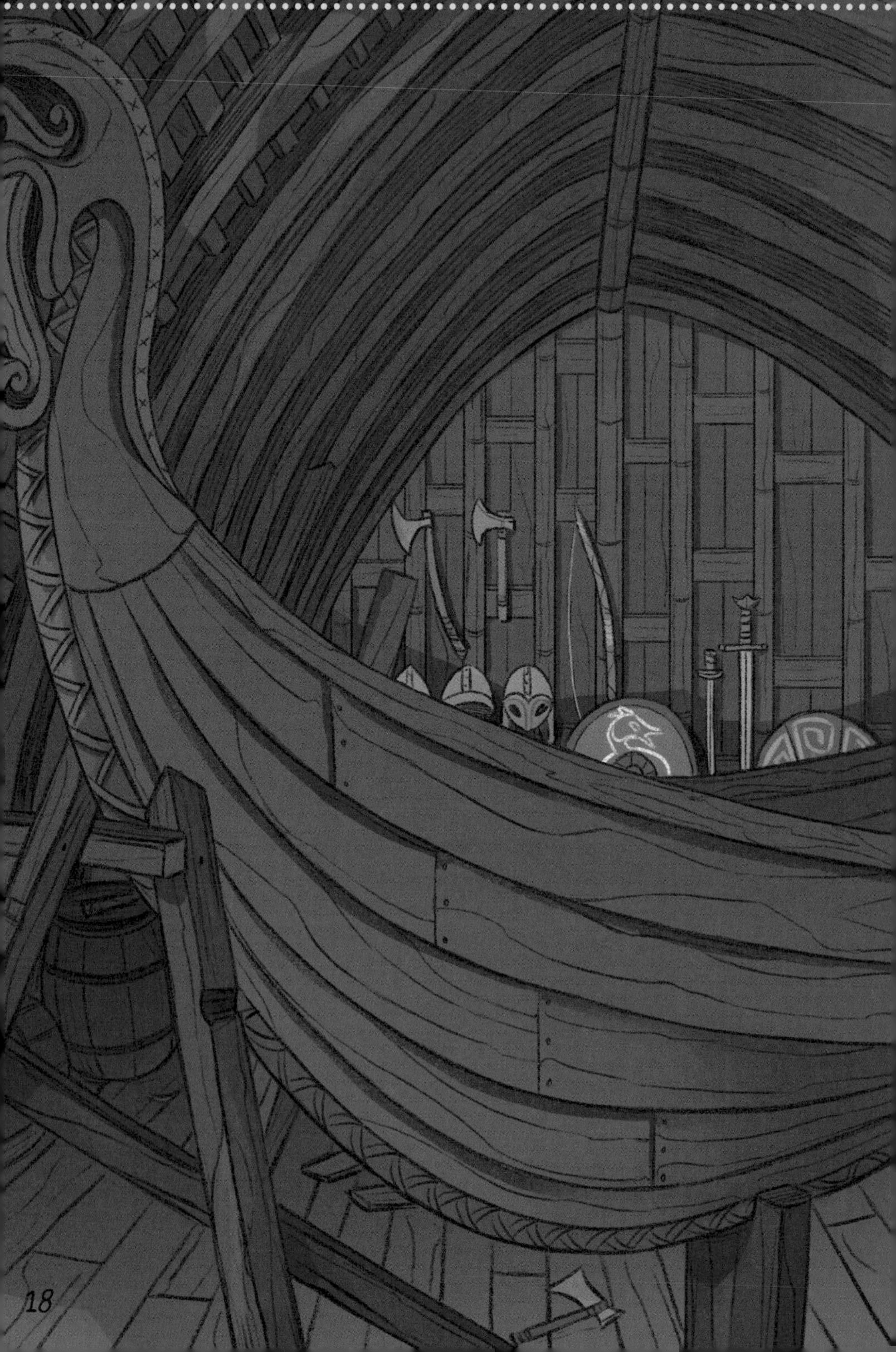

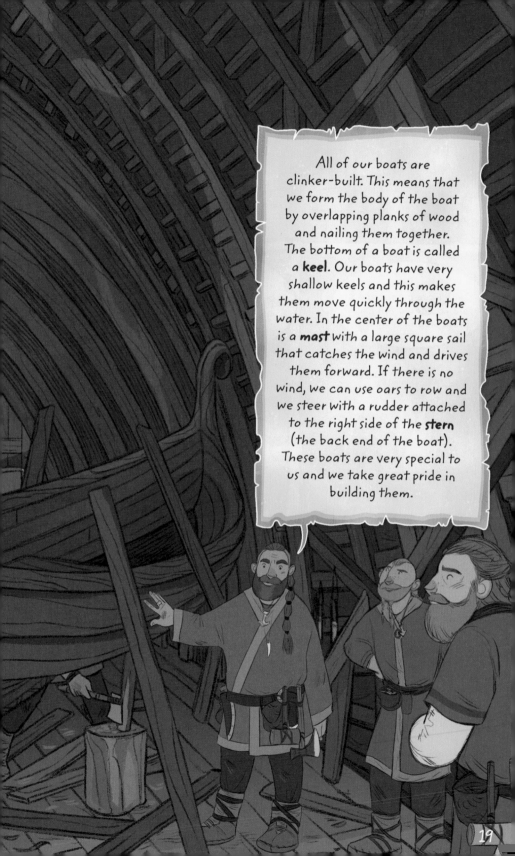

All of our boats are clinker-built. This means that we form the body of the boat by overlapping planks of wood and nailing them together. The bottom of a boat is called a **keel**. Our boats have very shallow keels and this makes them move quickly through the water. In the center of the boats is a **mast** with a large square sail that catches the wind and drives them forward. If there is no wind, we can use oars to row and we steer with a rudder attached to the right side of the **stern** (the back end of the boat). These boats are very special to us and we take great pride in building them.

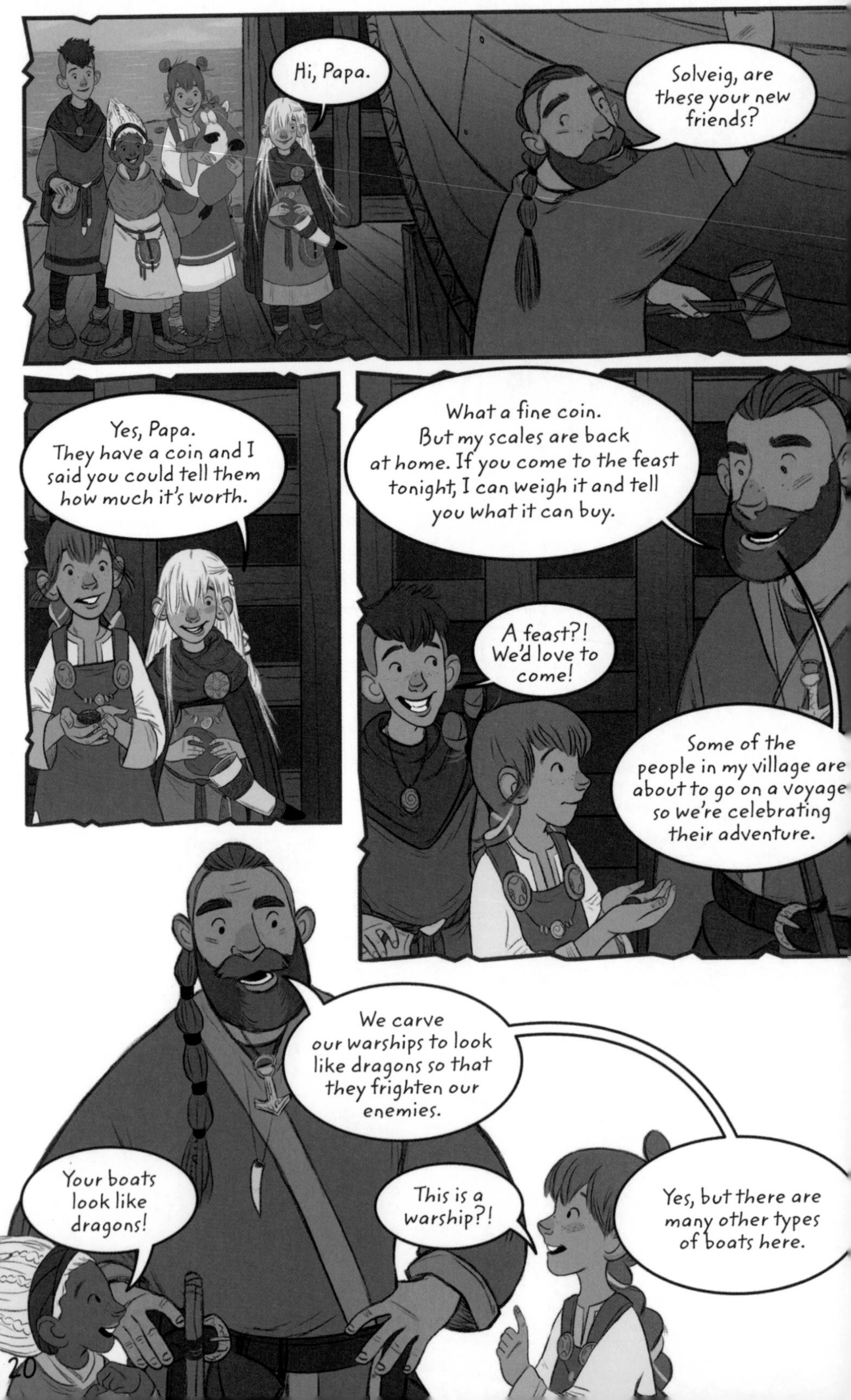

Hi, Papa.
Solveig, are these your new friends?
Yes, Papa. They have a coin and I said you could tell them how much it's worth.
What a fine coin. But my scales are back at home. If you come to the feast tonight, I can weigh it and tell you what it can buy.
A feast?! We'd love to come!
Some of the people in my village are about to go on a voyage so we're celebrating their adventure.
We carve our warships to look like dragons so that they frighten our enemies.
Your boats look like dragons!
This is a warship?!
Yes, but there are many other types of boats here.

Types of Viking Ships

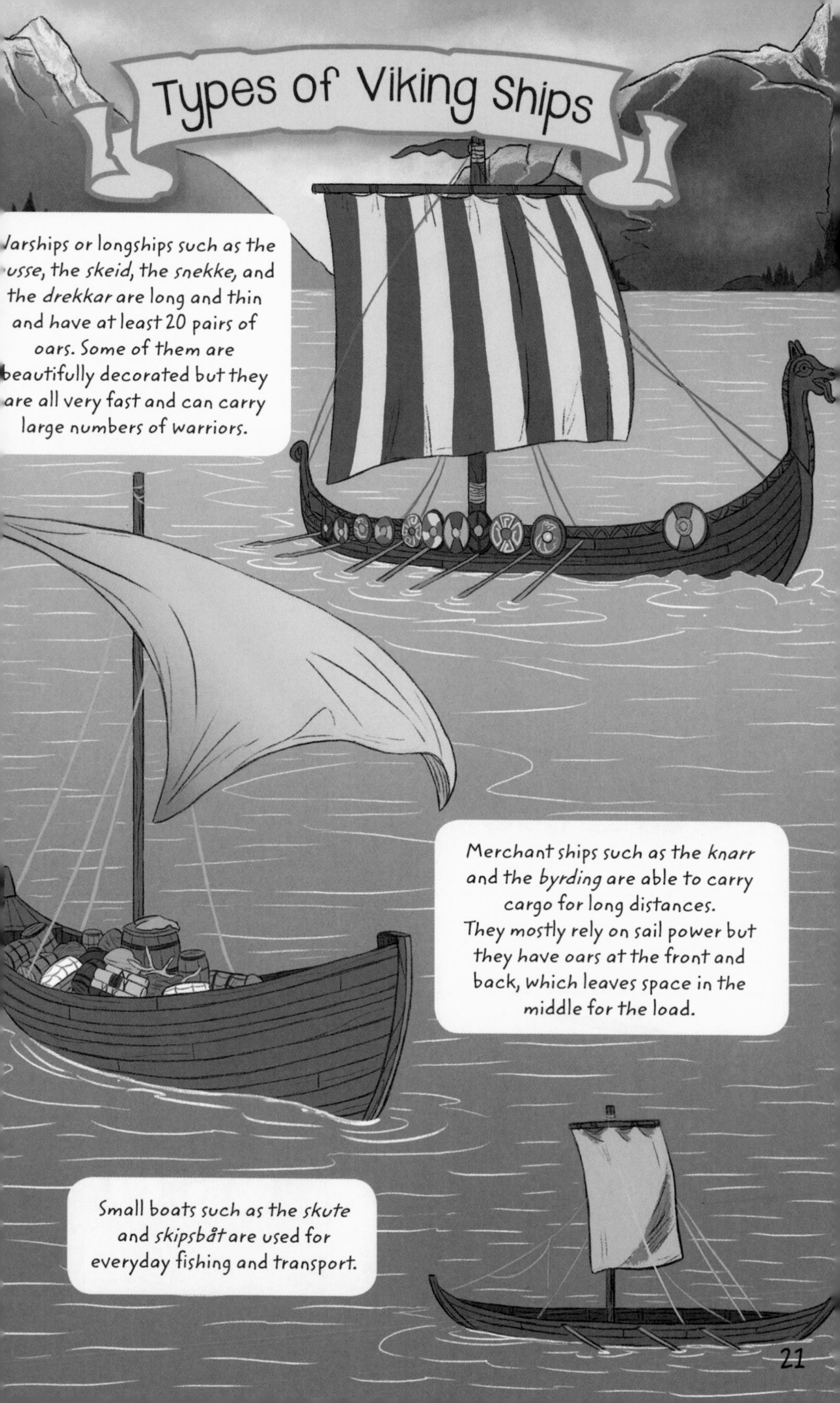

arships or longships such as the usse, the *skeid*, the *snekke*, and the *drekkar* are long and thin and have at least 20 pairs of oars. Some of them are beautifully decorated but they are all very fast and can carry large numbers of warriors.

Merchant ships such as the *knarr* and the *byrding* are able to carry cargo for long distances. They mostly rely on sail power but they have oars at the front and back, which leaves space in the middle for the load.

Small boats such as the *skute* and *skipsbåt* are used for everyday fishing and transport.

How to draw a Viking longboat

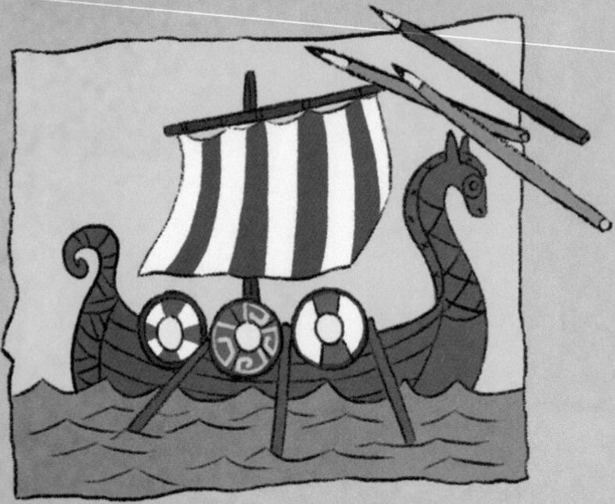

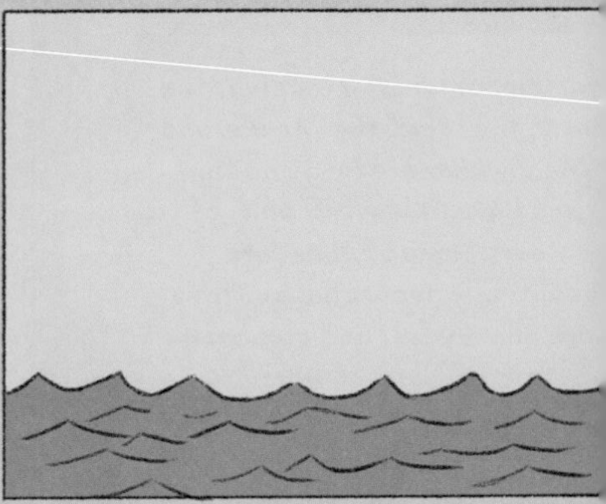

1. Draw some waves.

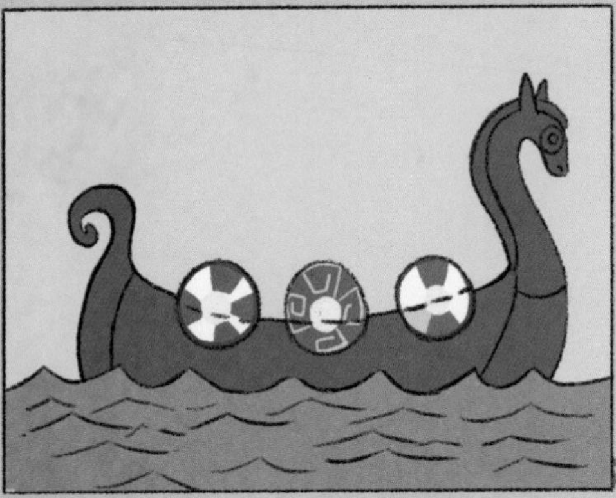

4. Draw three circles and rub out the boat's line.

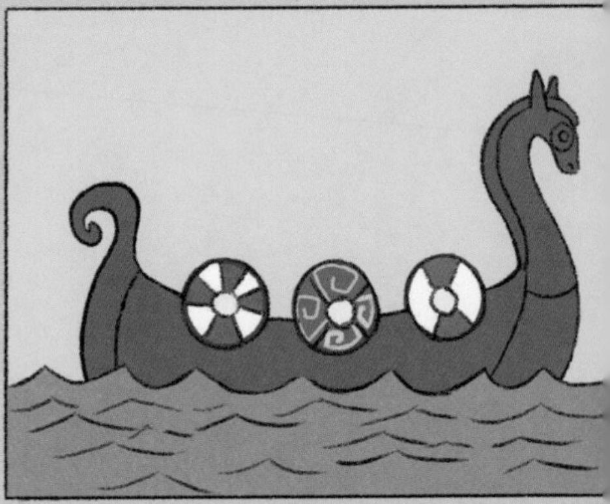

5. Draw a mini circle inside each big circle and decorate your shields.

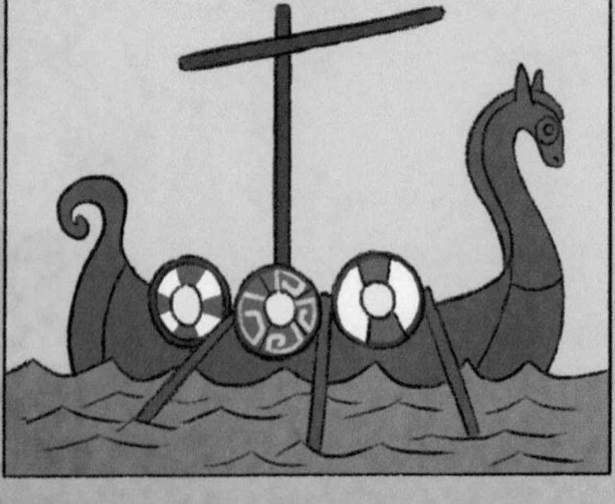

8. Draw another pole and erase inside.

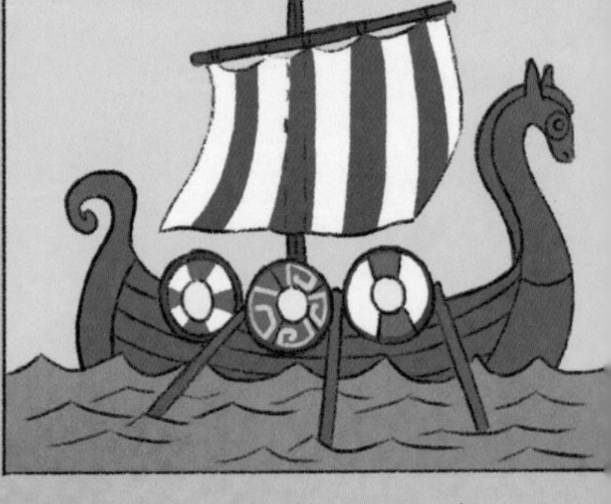

9. Draw a big sail and erase inside.

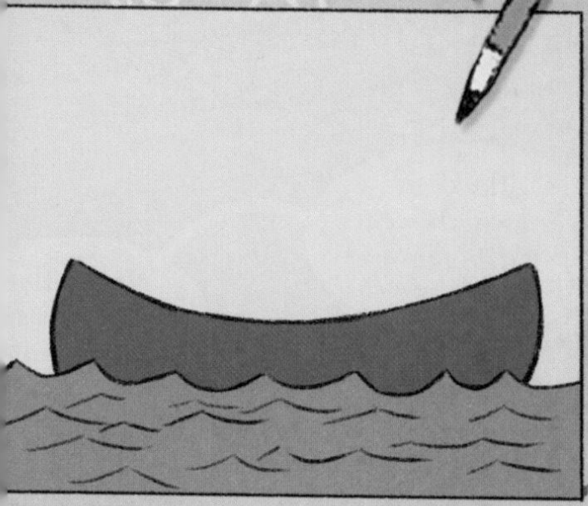

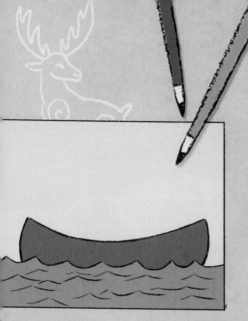

2. Draw a bowl shape.

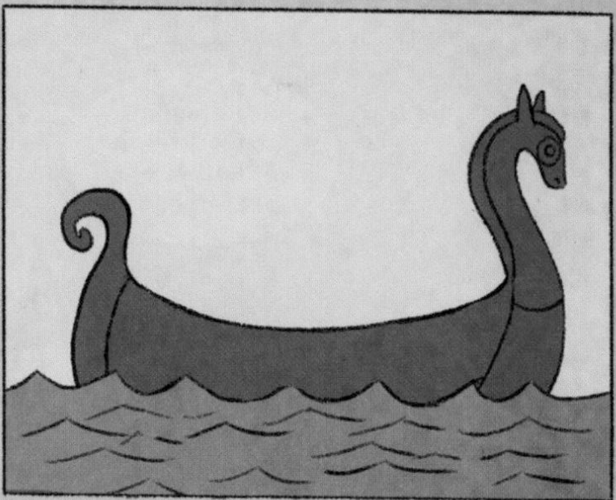

3. Give the bowl shape an amazing dragon head and tail.

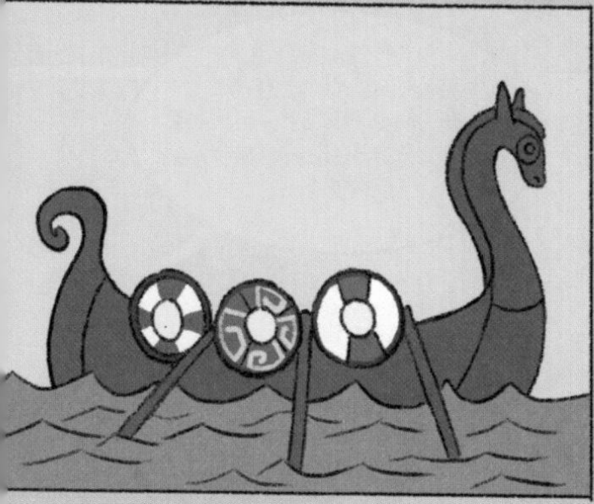

. Draw some lines for the oars.

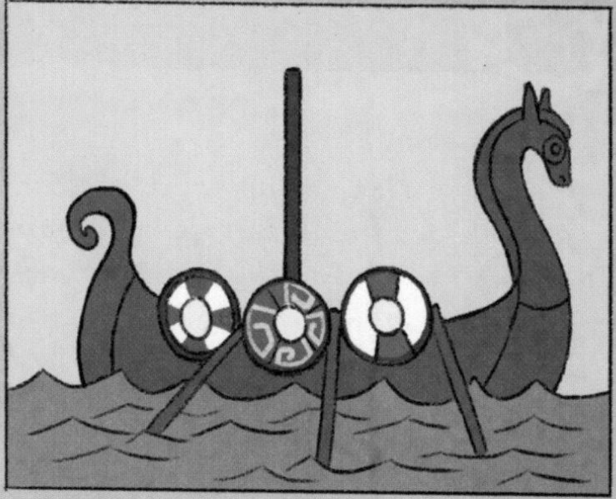

7. Draw a pole.

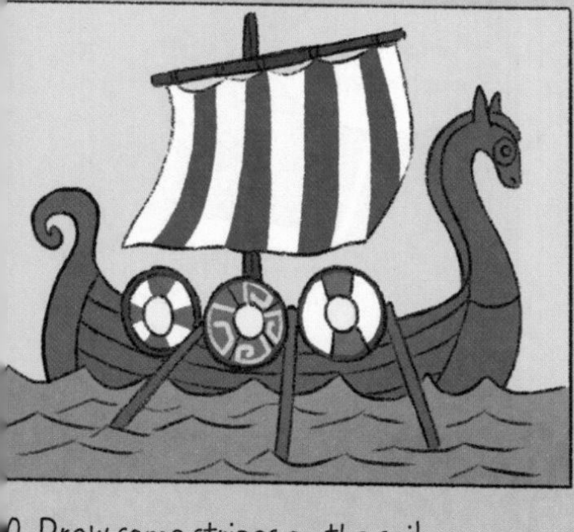

0. Draw some stripes on the sail.

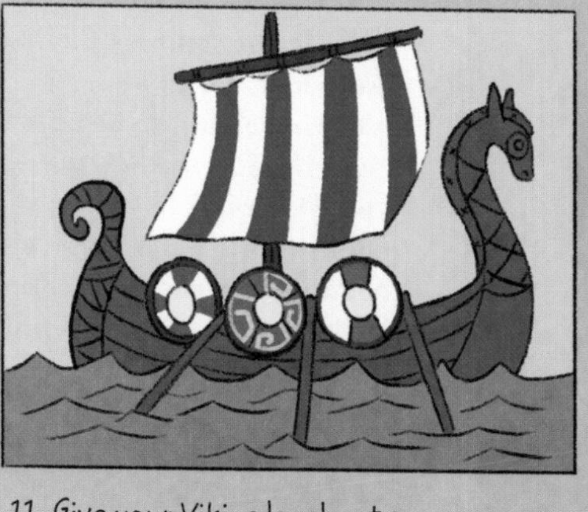

11. Give your Viking longboat some amazing decorations!

Viking navigation

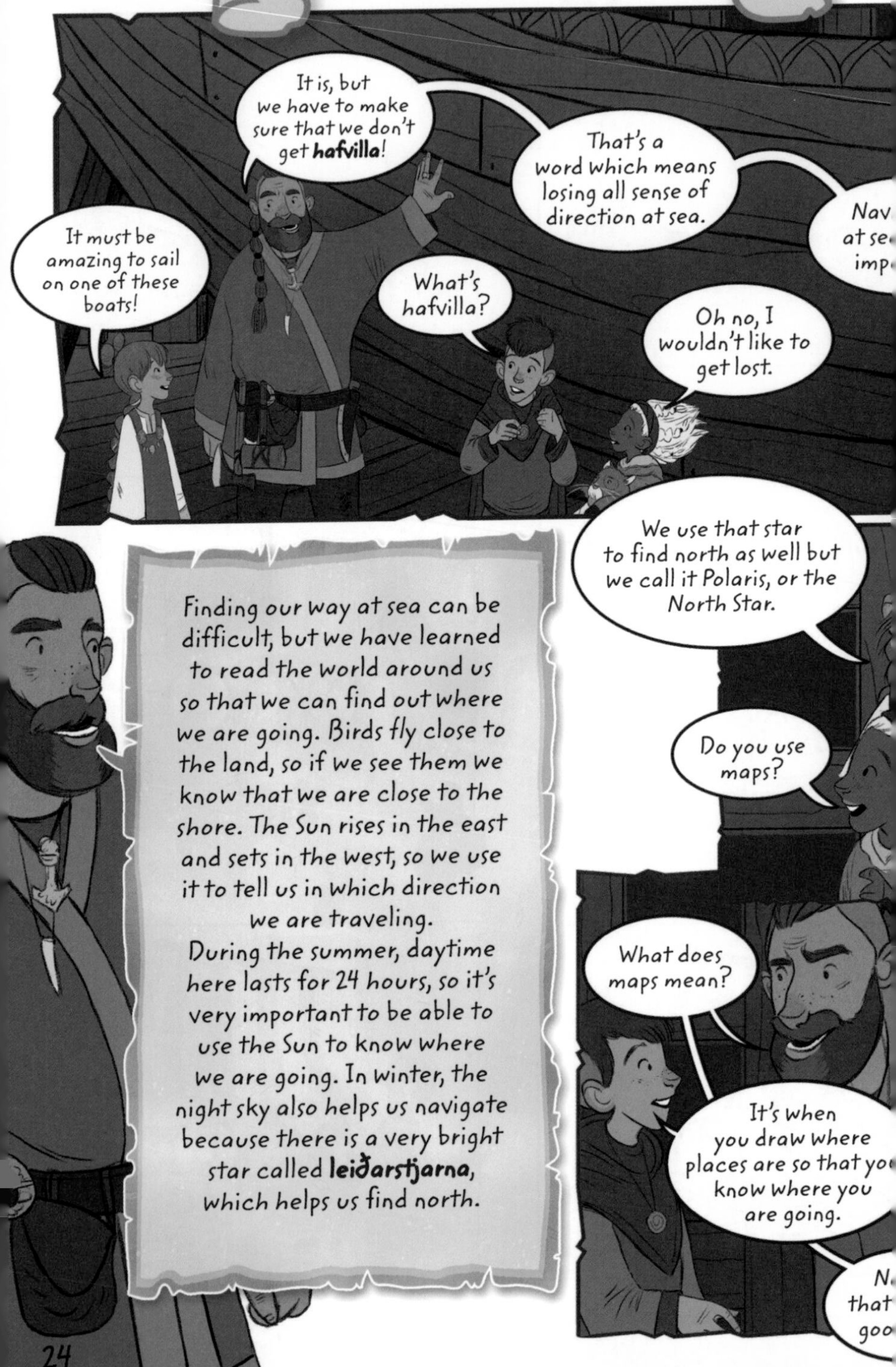
It must be amazing to sail on one of these boats!
It is, but we have to make sure that we don't get **hafvilla**!
What's hafvilla?
That's a word which means losing all sense of direction at sea.
Oh no, I wouldn't like to get lost.
Finding our way at sea can be difficult, but we have learned to read the world around us so that we can find out where we are going. Birds fly close to the land, so if we see them we know that we are close to the shore. The Sun rises in the east and sets in the west, so we use it to tell us in which direction we are traveling.
During the summer, daytime here lasts for 24 hours, so it's very important to be able to use the Sun to know where we are going. In winter, the night sky also helps us navigate because there is a very bright star called **leiðarstjarna**, which helps us find north.
We use that star to find north as well but we call it Polaris, or the North Star.
Do you use maps?
What does maps mean?
It's when you draw where places are so that yo
know where you are going.

Modern navigation research

Modern historians and scientists continue to research and experiment to find out about the tools that the Vikings used to help them navigate at sea. There is still very little archaeological evidence of Viking navigational instruments. Some researchers think that they might have used a magnetized piece of rock called a *lodestone* to make a compass.

Another theory is that the Vikings made compasses by keeping track of shadows cast by the Sun at different times of the day. There is also research into the existence of a sunstone, which was a piece of crystal that could be held up to a cloudy sky to help find the Sun by a process called *polarization*.

Make a "lodestone" magnetic compass

Ask a grown-up before using the needle!

You will need:

A large sewing needle
A magnet
A metal object, such as a paperclip or a screw
A bottle cap or a cork
Tape
A bowl or bucket of water

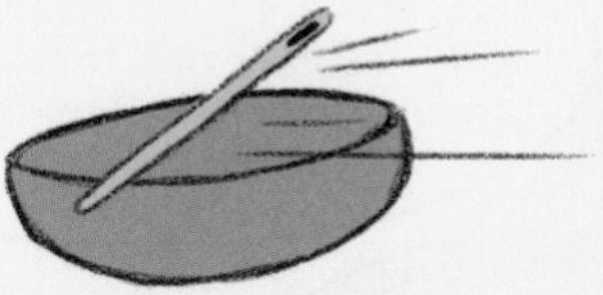

1. Holding the needle very carefully, swipe it along the side of the magnet repeatedly to make it magnetic. Forty or fifty times should be plenty.

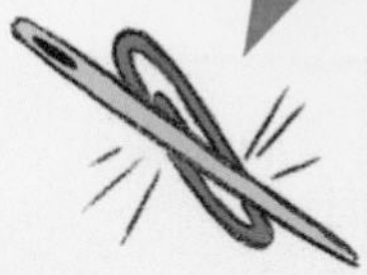

2. Use the metal object to test whether this has worked. If the needle sticks to it, you have made the needle magnetic. If not, try rubbing the needle along the magnet again.

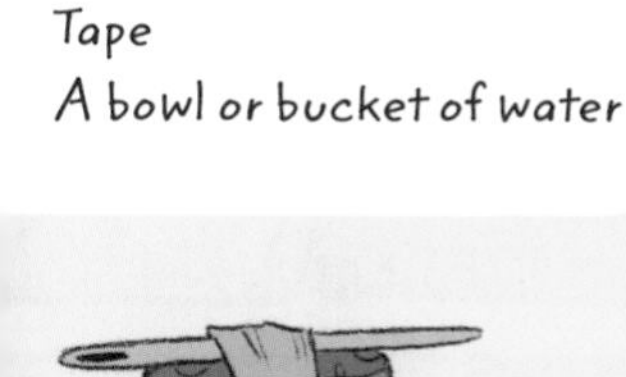

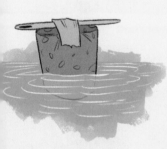

. Once the needle has been nagnetized, tape it to the op of the bottle cap or cork nd place it into the bowl of vater.

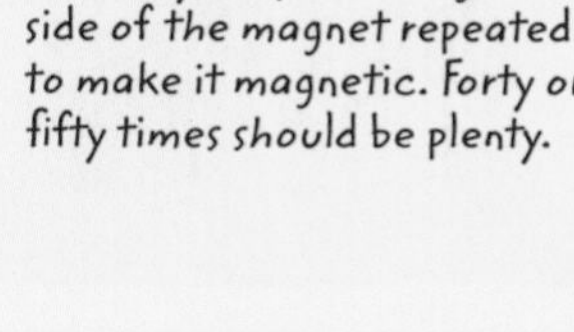

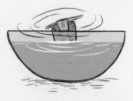

4. Let the needle spin. When it finally settles, it will point north.

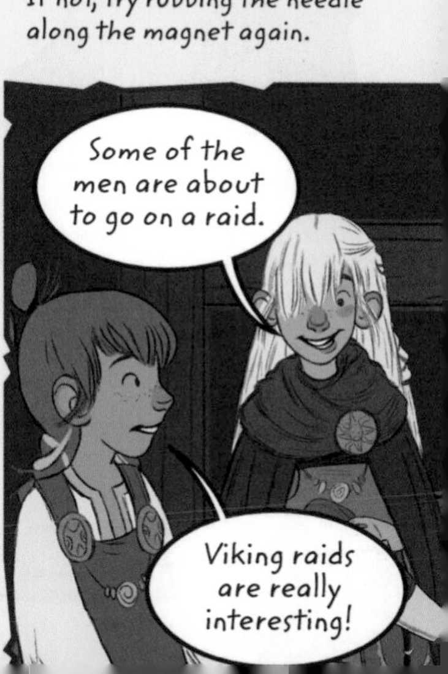
Some of the men are about to go on a raid.
Viking raids are really interesting!

Hero joins a Viking raid

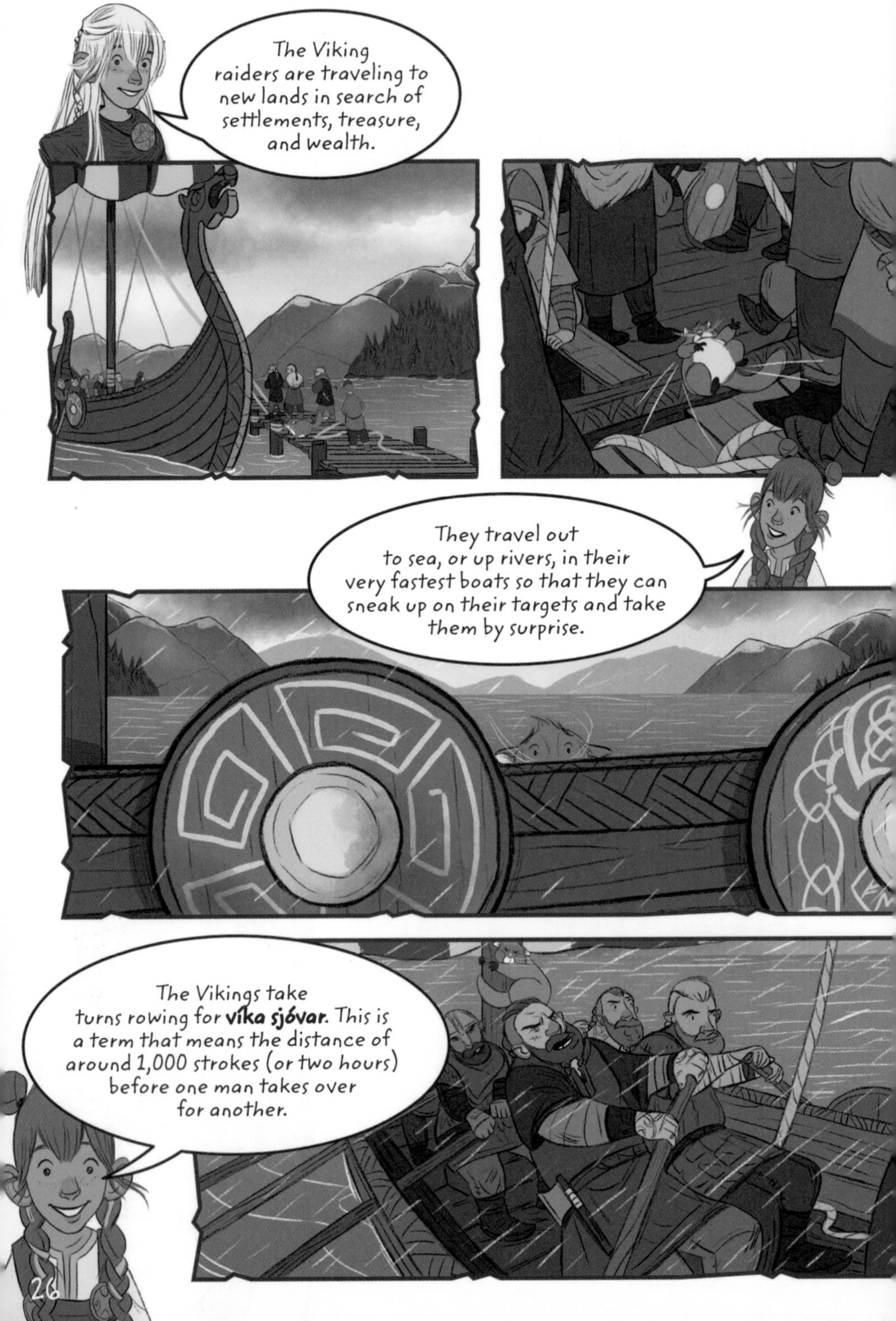
The Viking raiders are traveling to new lands in search of settlements, treasure, and wealth.
They travel out to sea, or up rivers, in their very fastest boats so that they can sneak up on their targets and take them by surprise.
The Vikings take turns rowing for **víka sjóvar**. This is a term that means the distance of around 1,000 strokes (or two hours) before one man takes over for another.

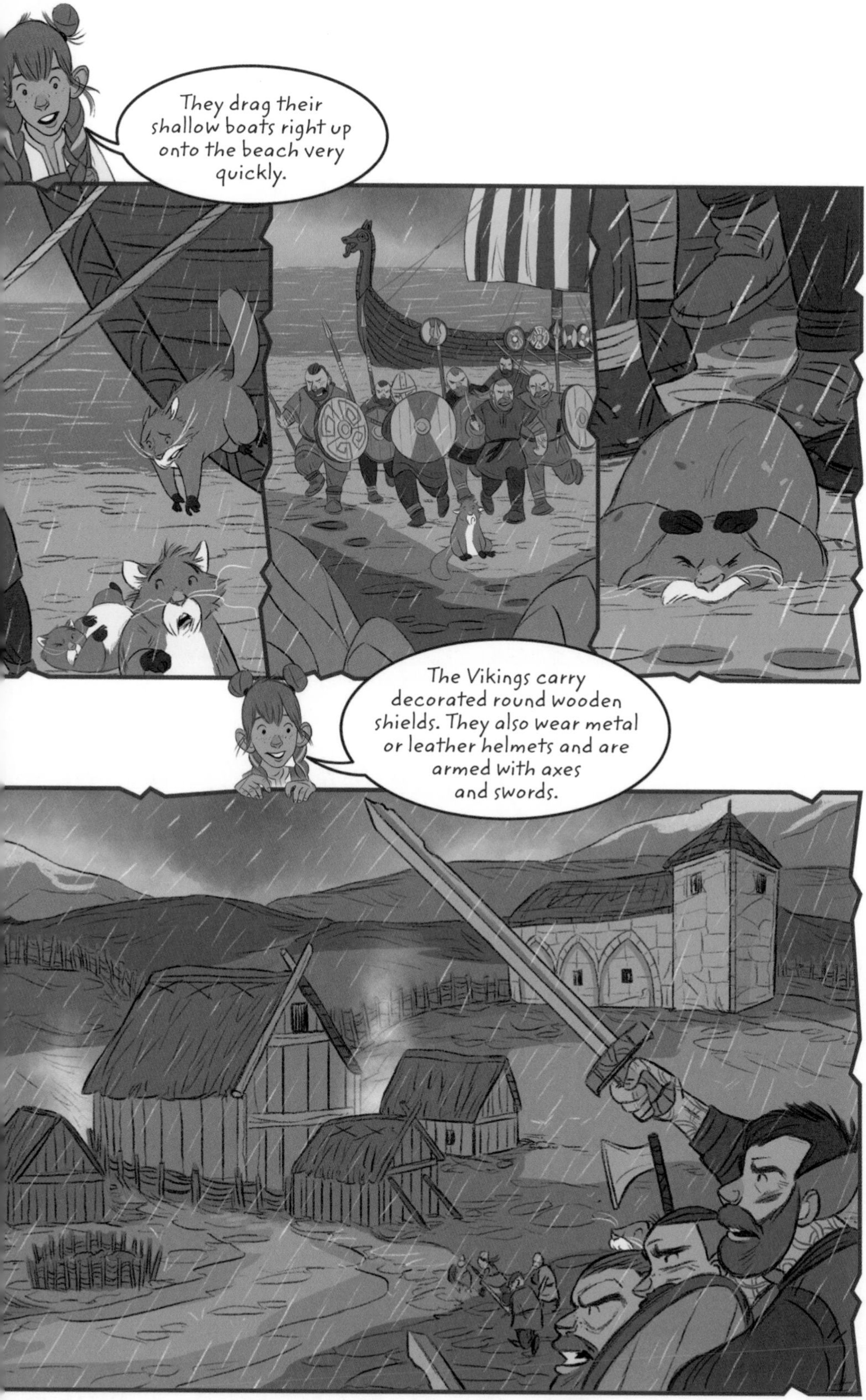
They drag their shallow boats right up onto the beach very quickly.
The Vikings carry decorated round wooden shields. They also wear metal or leather helmets and are armed with axes and swords.

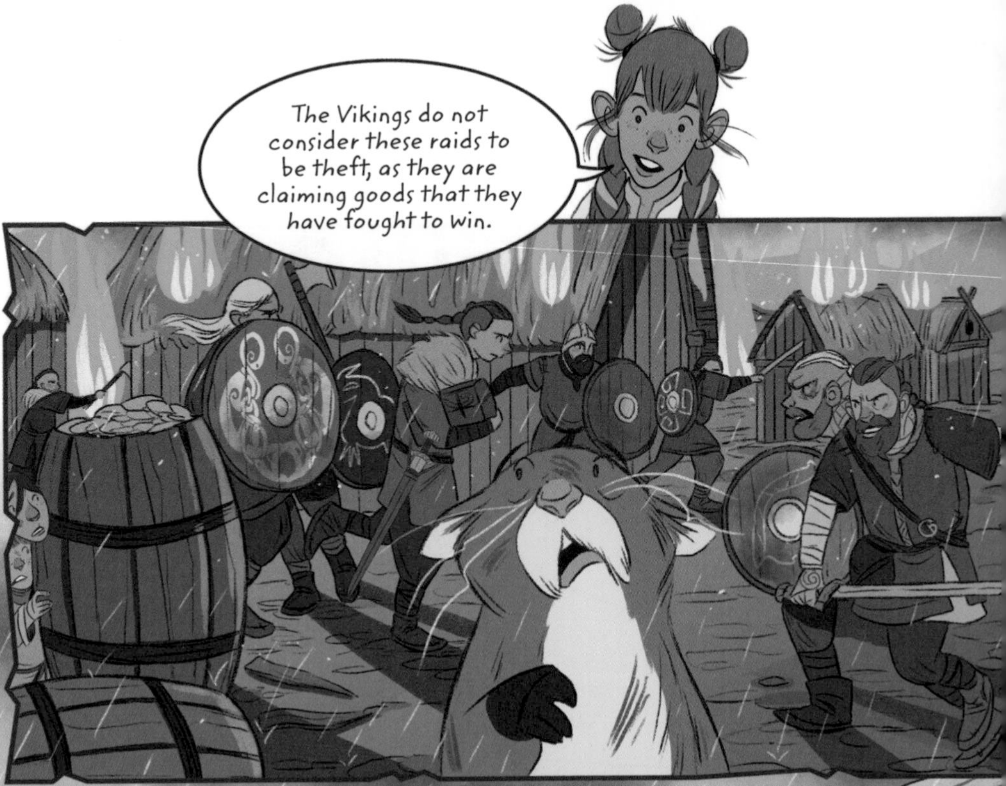
The Vikings do not consider these raids to be theft, as they are claiming goods that they have fought to win.

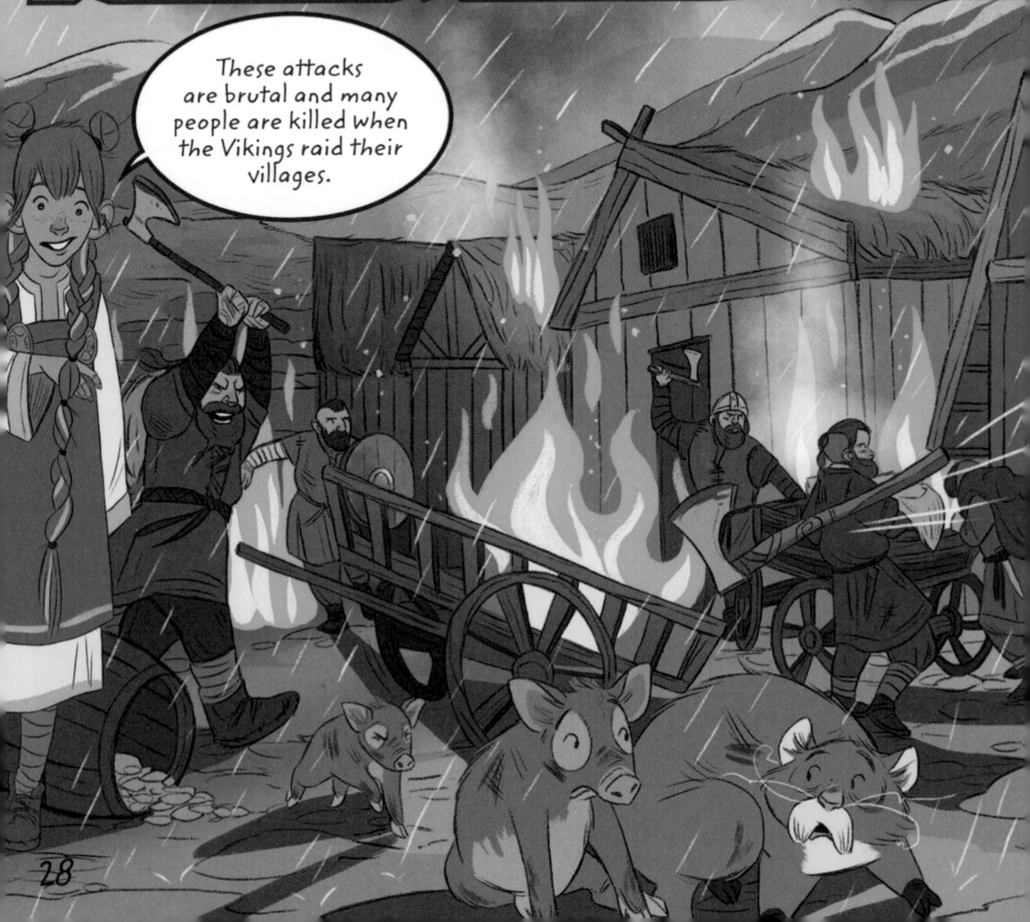
These attacks are brutal and many people are killed when the Vikings raid their villages.

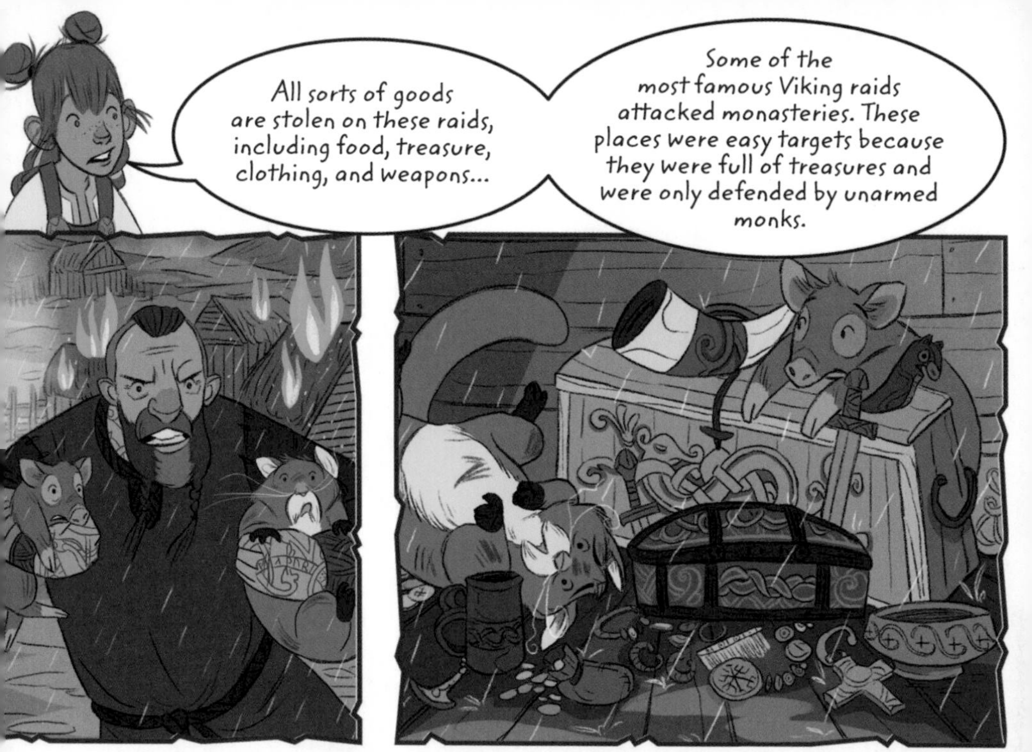
All sorts of goods are stolen on these raids, including food, treasure, clothing, and weapons...
Some of the most famous Viking raids attacked monasteries. These places were easy targets because they were full of treasures and were only defended by unarmed monks.

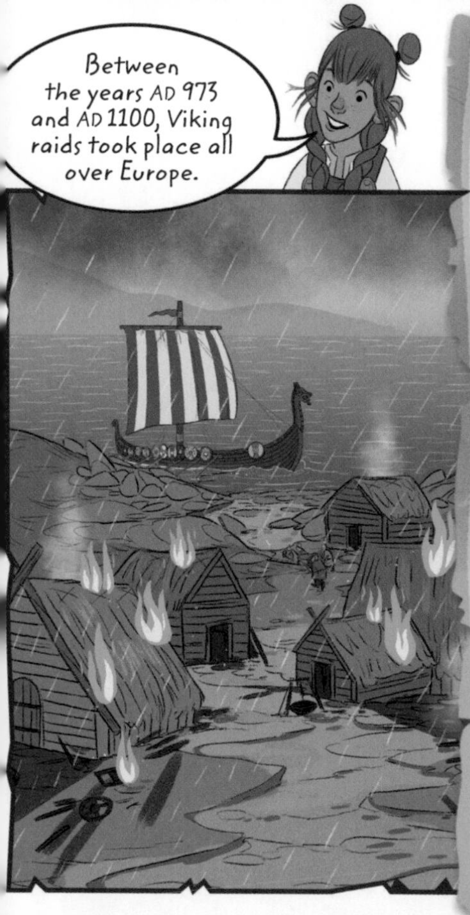
Between the years AD 973 and AD 1100, Viking raids took place all over Europe.

Viking property and social order

- One of the most valuable items that Vikings stole on their raids were people who, once kidnapped, were forced to become slaves.
- These enslaved people were considered property that could be bought or sold. The Vikings traded slaves all over the world.
- These slaves were called **thralls** and they were one of the Norse social classes.
- The social classes included kings, **jarls**, **karls**, and thralls. A king or chief ruled over a region, a jarl was a member of the nobility, and a karl was a freeman who could own land, set up a business, and build property.
- Thralls might eventually be able to buy their freedom or be freed by their owner.

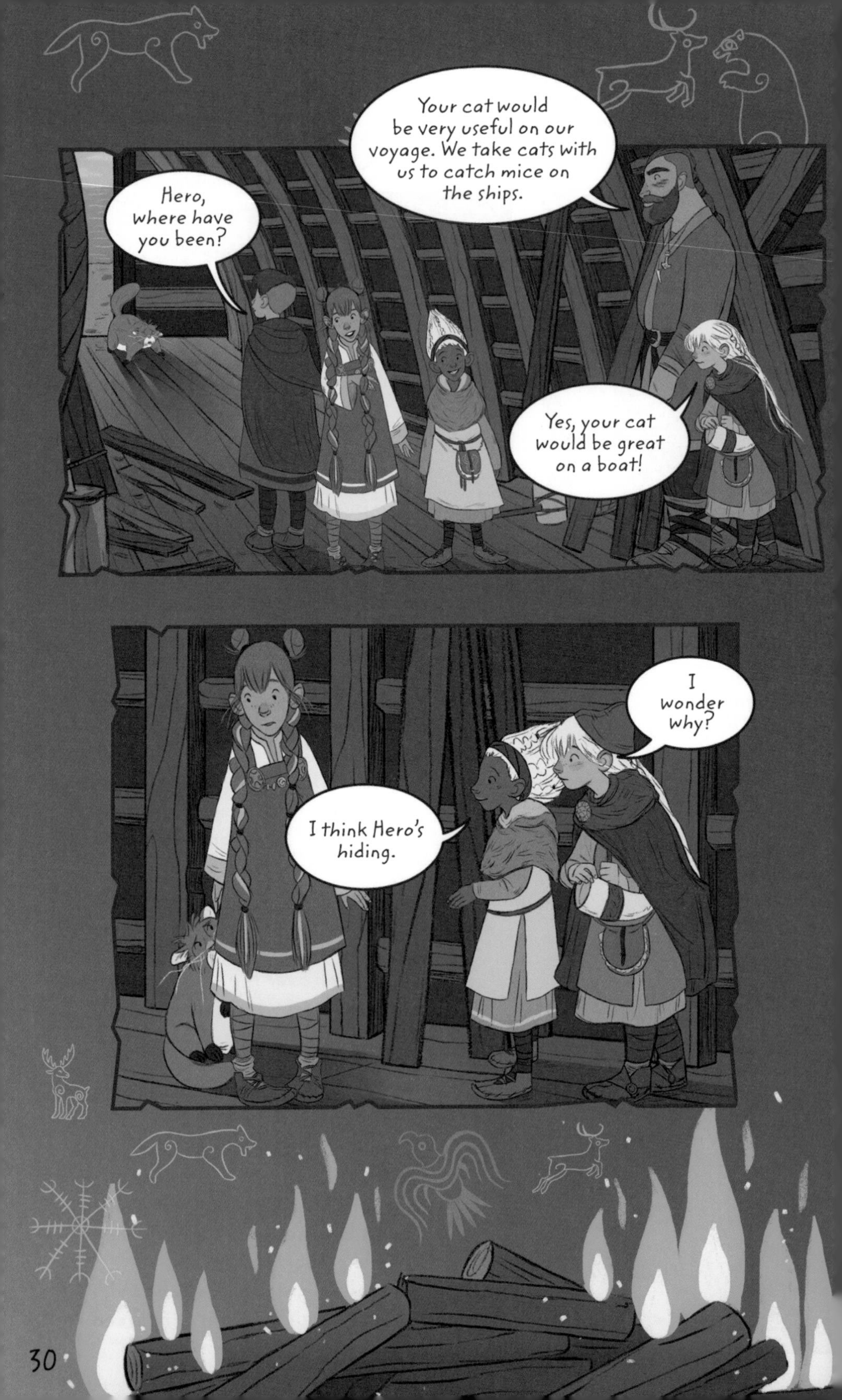
Hero, where have you been?
Your cat would be very useful on our voyage. We take cats with us to catch mice on the ships.
Yes, your cat would be great on a boat!
I think Hero's hiding.
I wonder why?

Viking boat burials

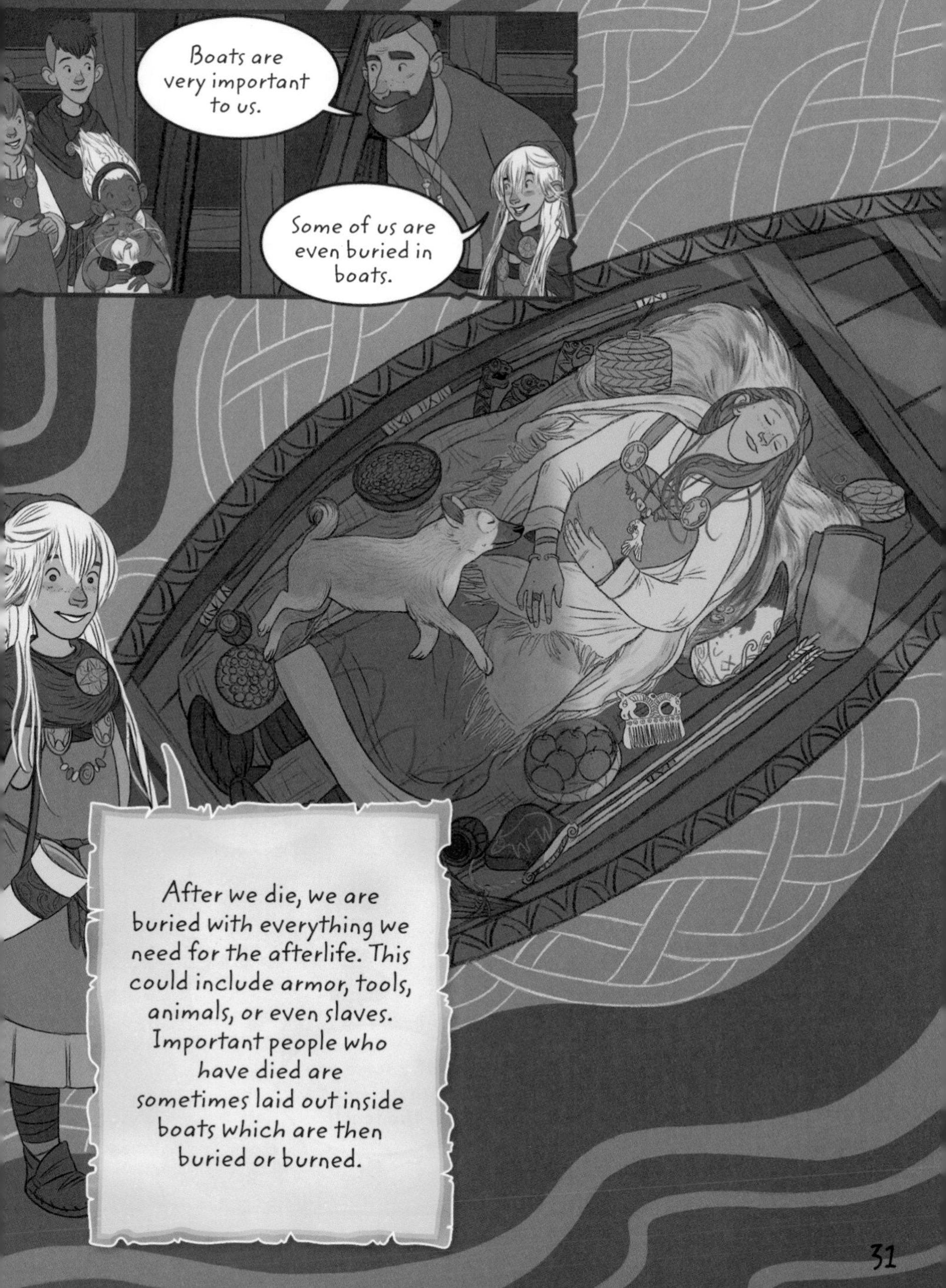

Boats are very important to us.
Some of us are even buried in boats.
After we die, we are buried with everything we need for the afterlife. This could include armor, tools, animals, or even slaves. Important people who have died are sometimes laid out inside boats which are then buried or burned.

Fishing, farming, and foraging

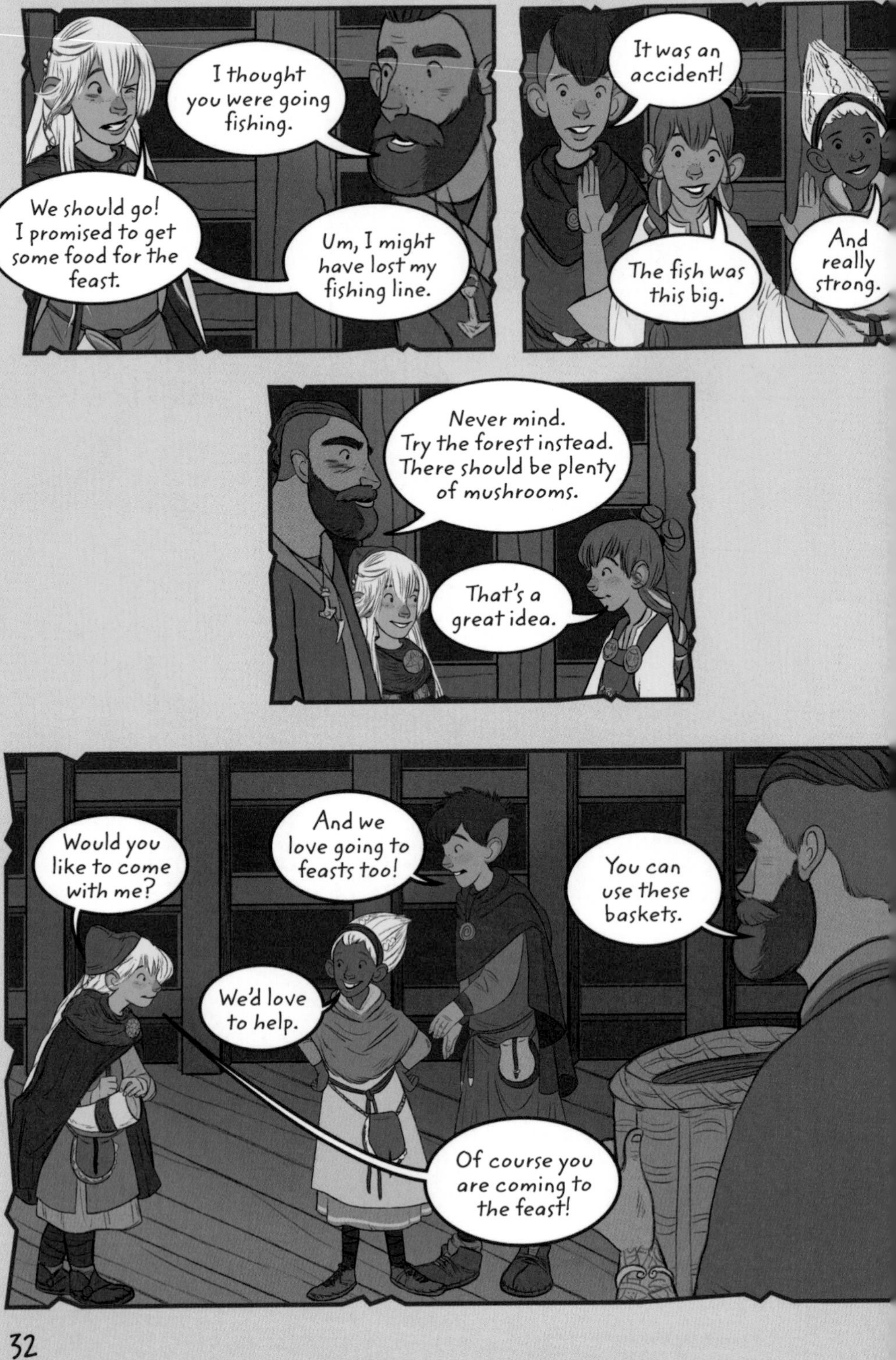

I thought you were going fishing.
We should go! I promised to get some food for the feast.
Um, I might have lost my fishing line.
It was an accident!
The fish was this big.
And really strong.
Never mind. Try the forest instead. There should be plenty of mushrooms.
That's a great idea.
Would you like to come with me?
And we love going to feasts too!
You can use these baskets.
We'd love to help.
Of course you are coming to the feast!

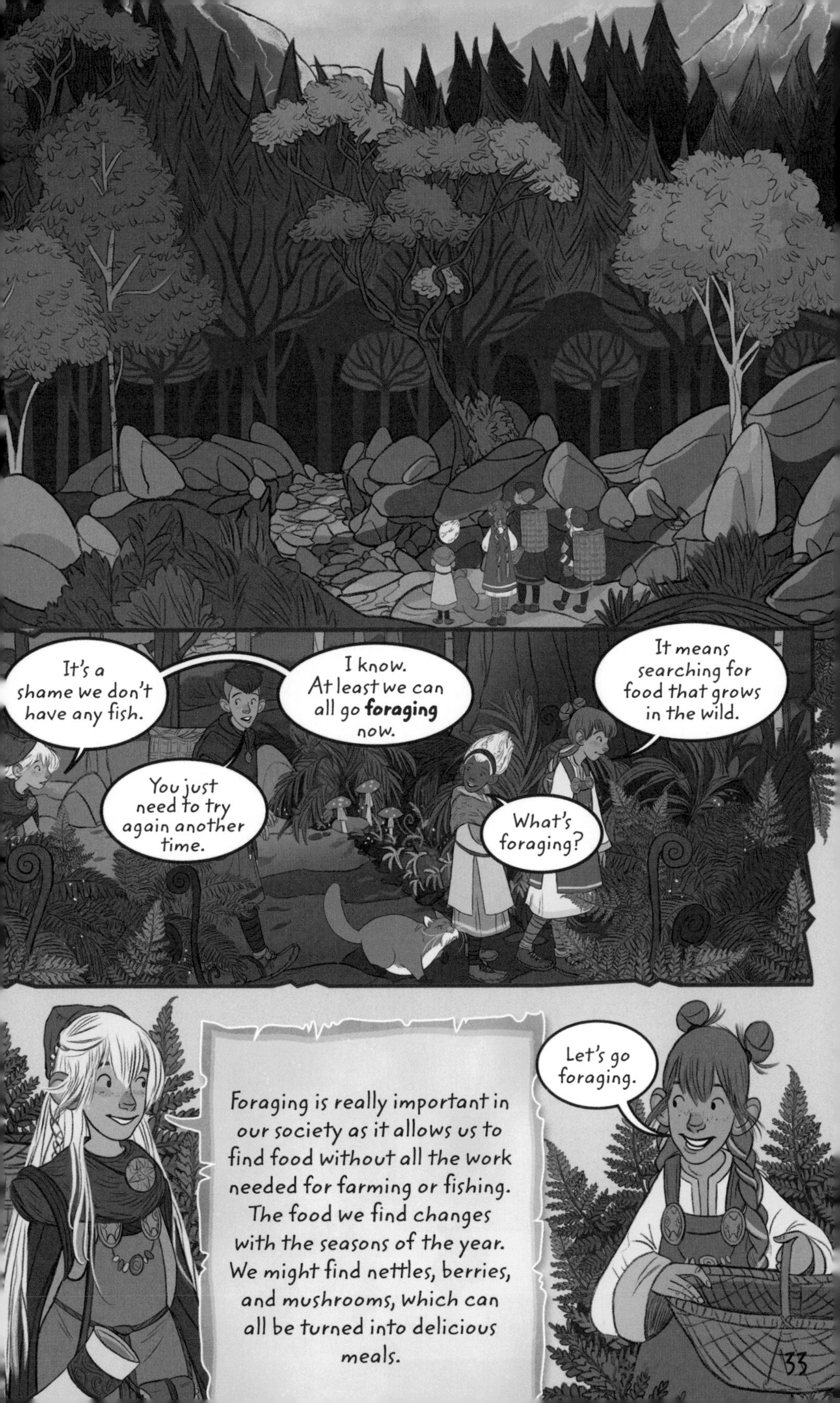
It's a shame we don't have any fish.
I know. At least we can all go **foraging** now.
You just need to try again another time.
What's foraging?
It means searching for food that grows in the wild.
Foraging is really important in our society as it allows us to find food without all the work needed for farming or fishing. The food we find changes with the seasons of the year. We might find nettles, berries, and mushrooms, which can all be turned into delicious meals.
Let's go foraging.

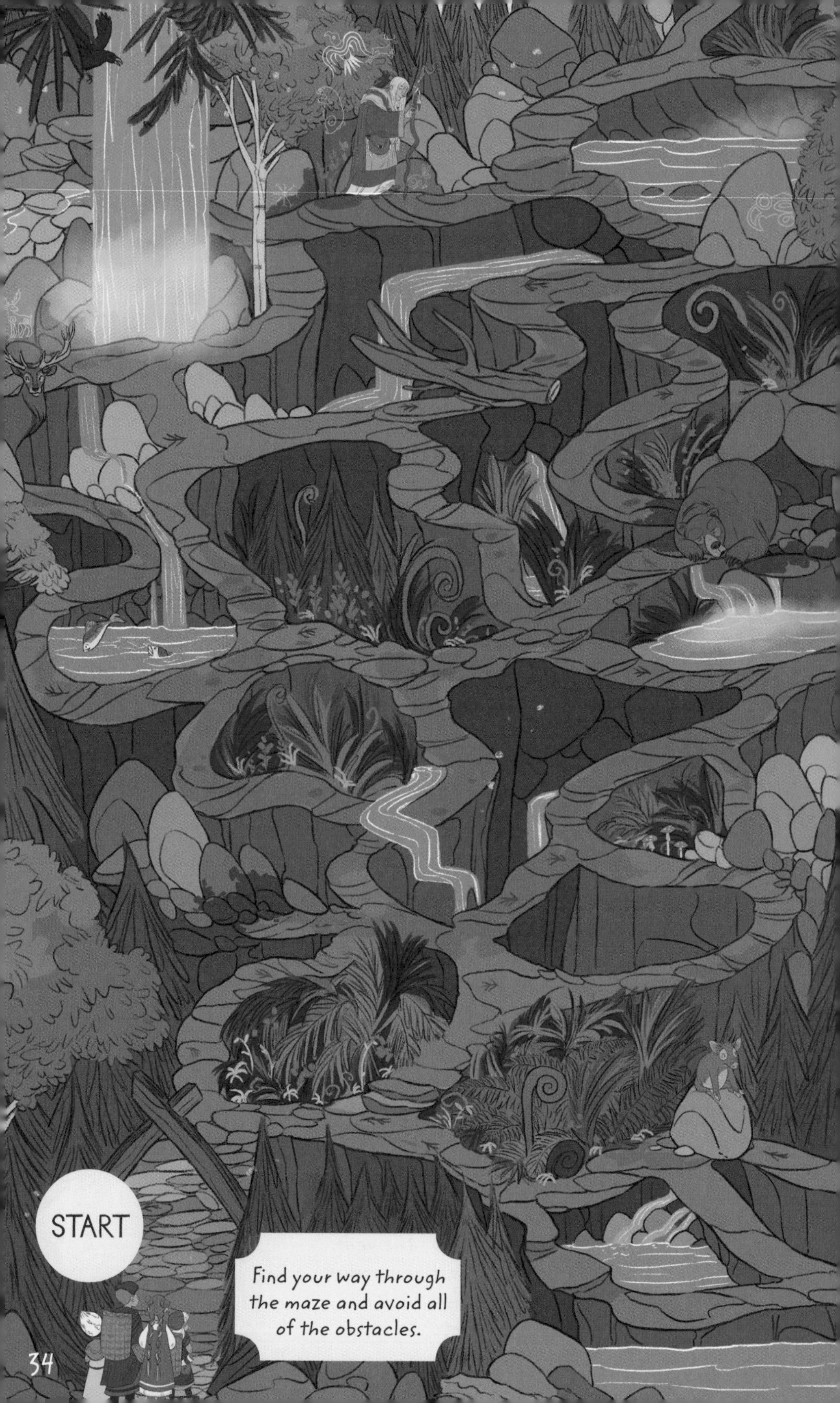
START
Find your way through the maze and avoid all of the obstacles.

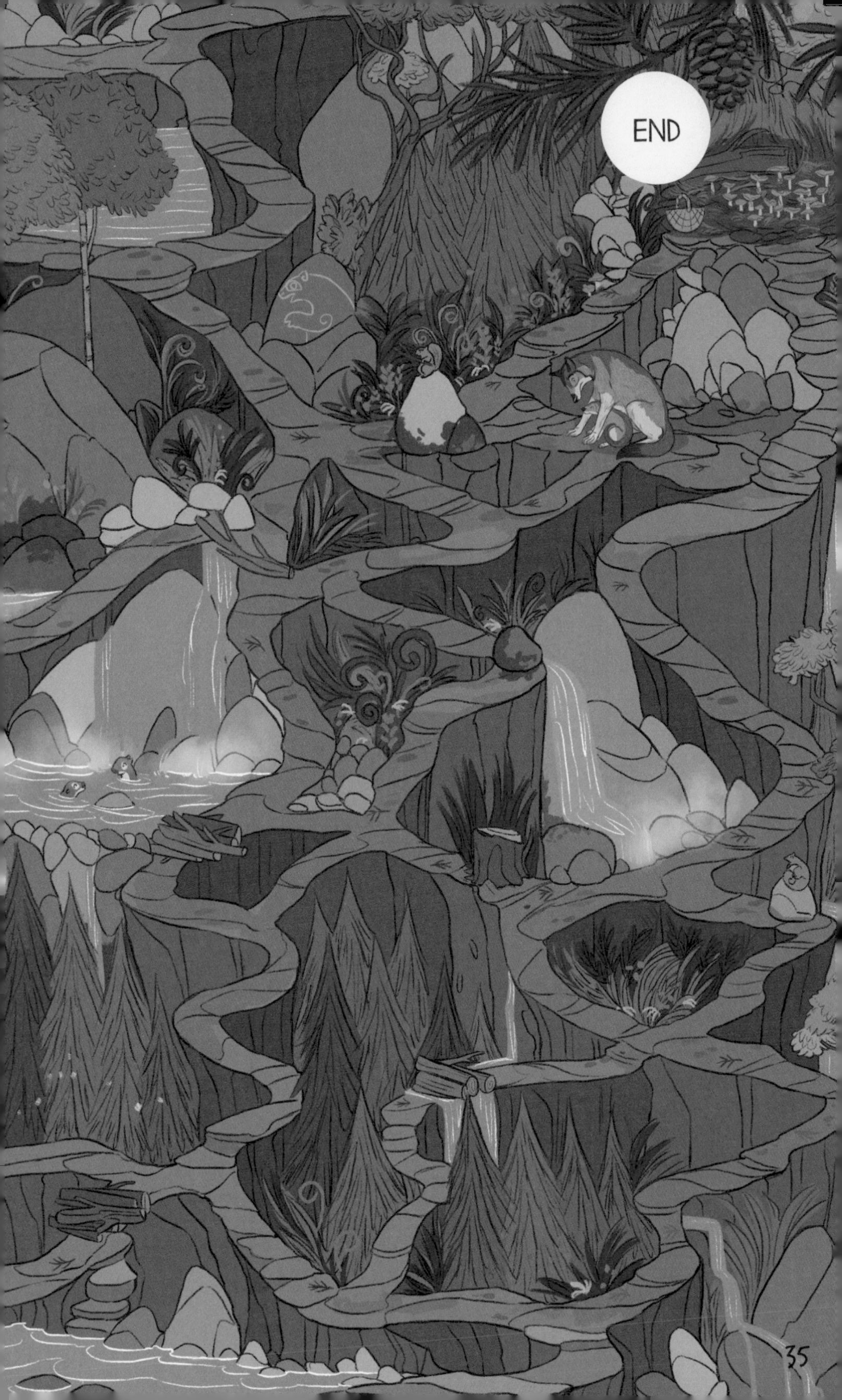
END

A visit to the farm

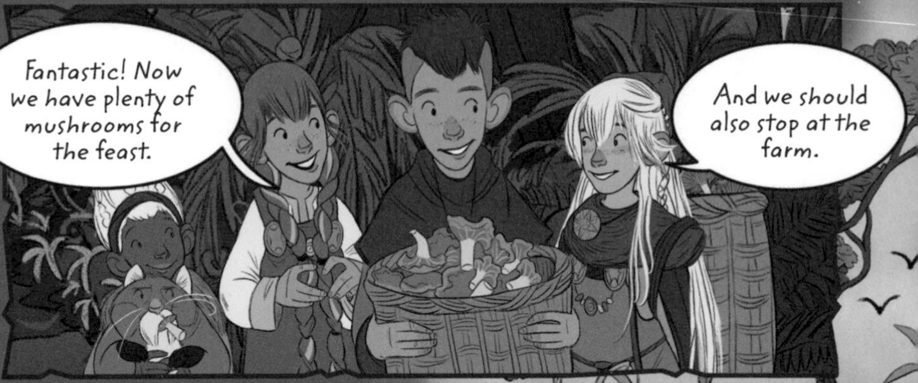
Fantastic! Now we have plenty of mushrooms for the feast.
And we should also stop at the farm.

Viking farming

- Viking farms grew plants for food, medicine, and dyeing cloth.
- Typical farm crops included oats, wheat, barley, and vegetables.
- Farming fields were usually found outside the main settlement.
- Farms also kept animals such as cows, sheep, hens, geese, and horses.
- During the early Viking period, animals would be kept inside the main longhouse.
- By the later Viking period, farms had grown bigger, so animals would be kept in outbuildings.

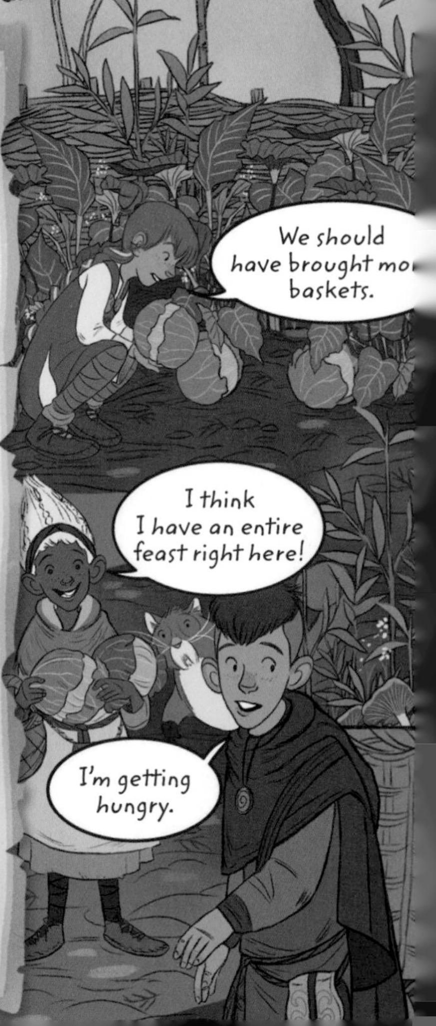
We should have brought mo baskets.
I think I have an entire feast right here!
I'm getting hungry.

A rune stone

Rune stones were large stone monuments that recorded the most heroic warriors and explorers. Vikings decorated the stones with very bright colors and wrote on them to remember brave deeds. The writing on these stones was made of symbols which are called **runes**. The runes could be written from left to right, right to left, and up and down.

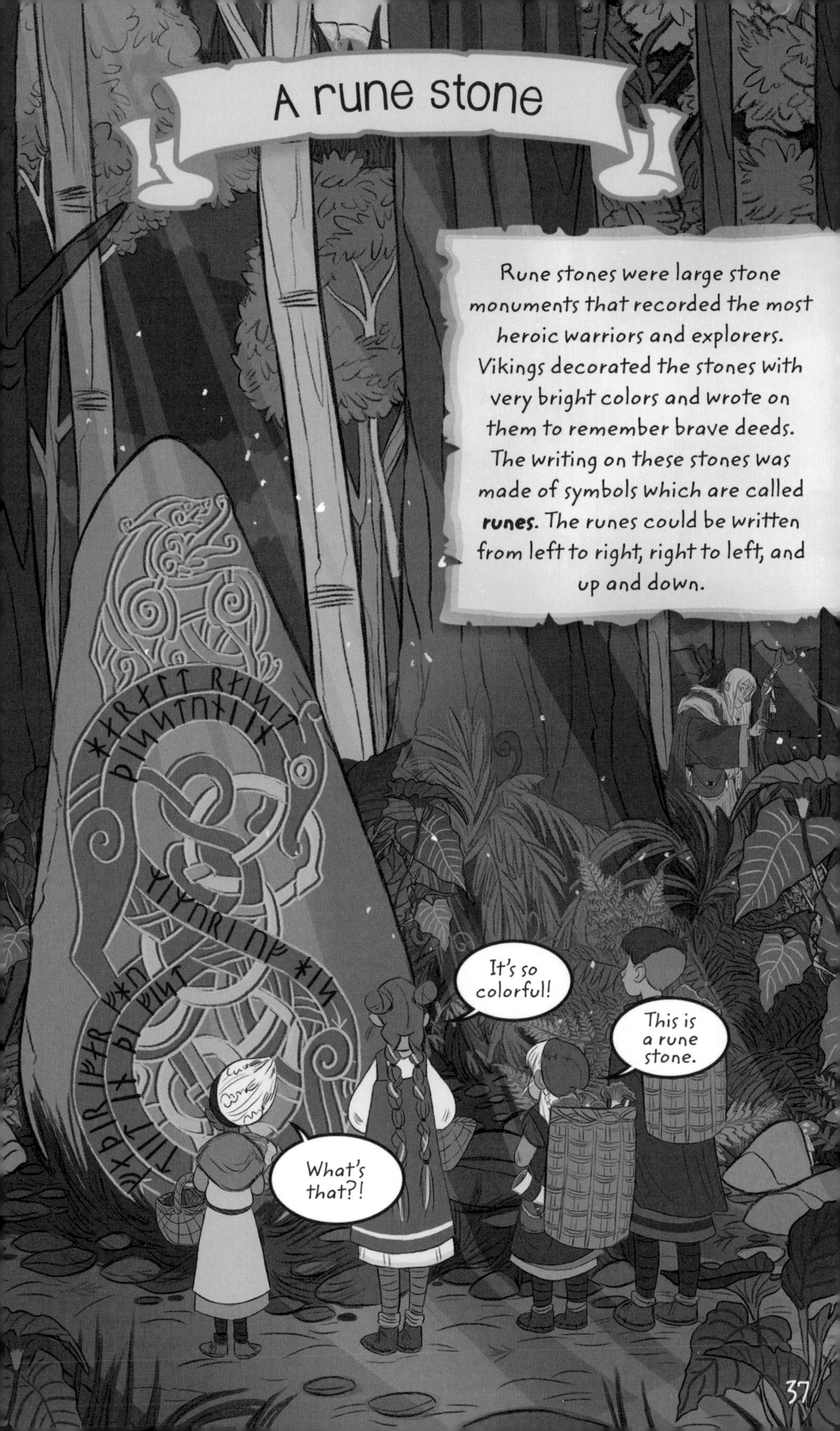
It's so colorful!
This is a rune stone.
What's that?!

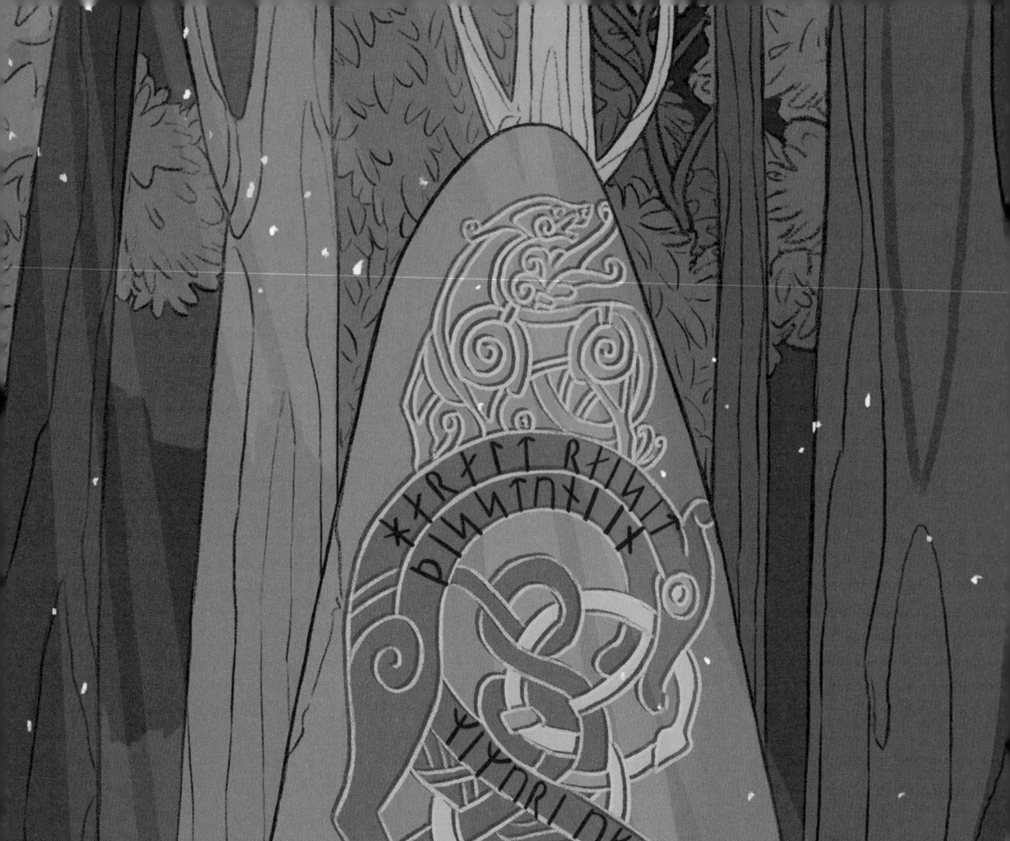

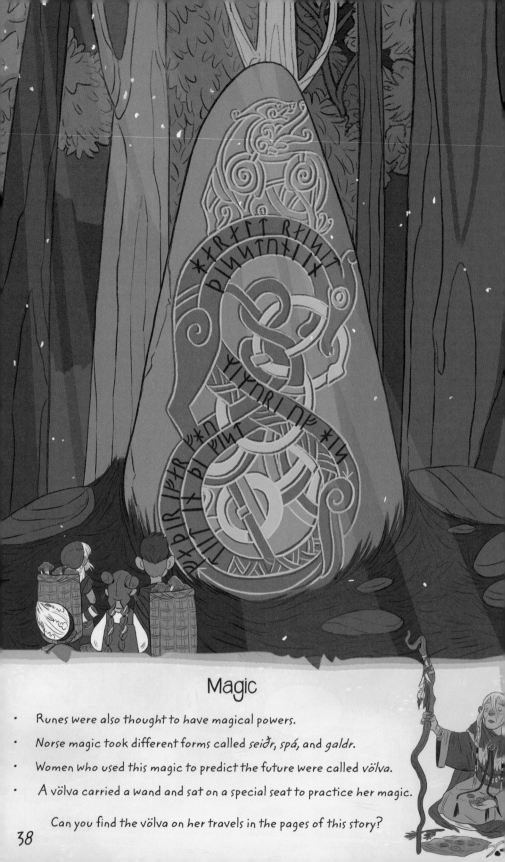

Magic

- Runes were also thought to have magical powers.
- Norse magic took different forms called *seiðr*, *spá*, and *galdr*.
- Women who used this magic to predict the future were called *völva*.
- A völva carried a wand and sat on a special seat to practice her magic.

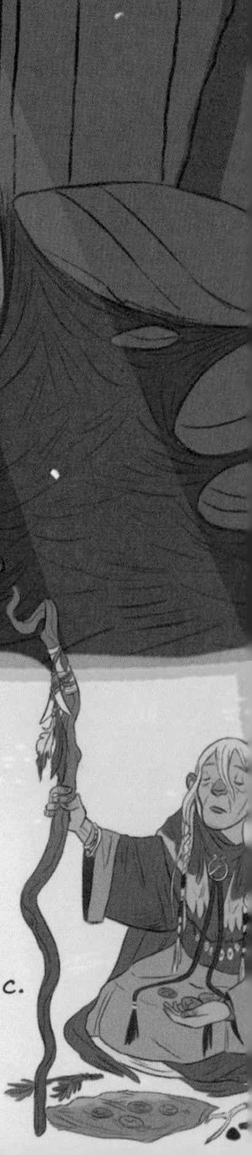

Can you find the völva on her travels in the pages of this story?

Runic alphabet

ᚠ	ᚢ	ᚦ	ᛉ	ᚱ	ᚴ	ᛪ	ᚼ
fvw	uo	th	ą	r	kcgq	h	n

ᛁ	ᛆ	ᛋ	ᛏ	ᛒ	ᚤ	ᛚ	ᛦ
iejy	a	sxz	td	bp	m	l	R

Runic writing

- The alphabet used to write Old Norse in Scandinavia up until around AD 700 was called *Elder Futhark*.
- There are 24 runic symbols in Elder Futhark.
- *Futhark* refers to the first six symbols of this alphabet.
- Each of these runes represents a spoken sound.
- Some of these symbols can be used for more than one similar sound.
- During the period of the Vikings, this alphabet became *Younger Futhark* and had only the 16 symbols you see here.
- It then increased again during the medieval period to 27 symbols.
- *Younger Futhark* was written in different ways in different parts of Scandinavia.
- Þ is a symbol called a *thorn*, which is pronounced "th."

Translate the rune stone on the opposite page.

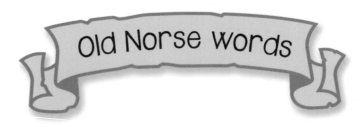

Old Norse Words

The Vikings spoke a language we call Old Norse.
They called this language **dönsk tunga**, which means the Danish tong
Many of the words that the Vikings used have developed into words t
appear in English today.

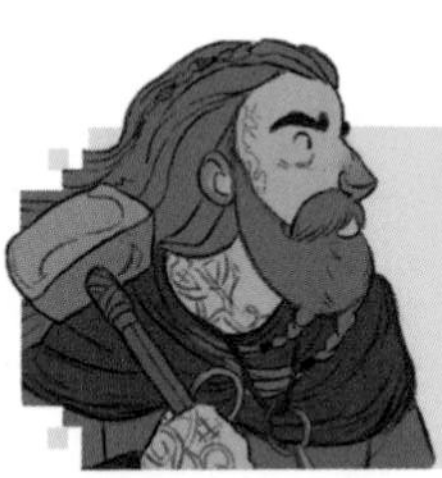

Þorsdagr
Thursday
(Thor's Day)

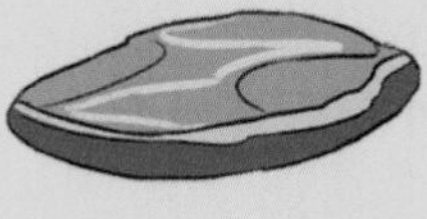

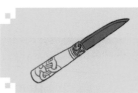

Steik
Steak

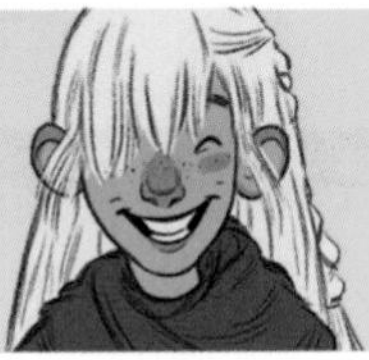

Happ
Happy

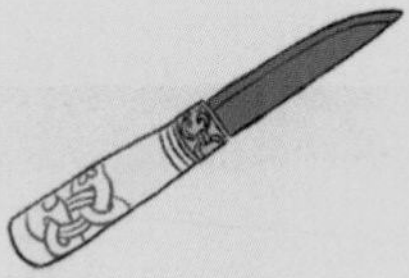

Knif
Knif

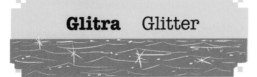

Glitra Glitter

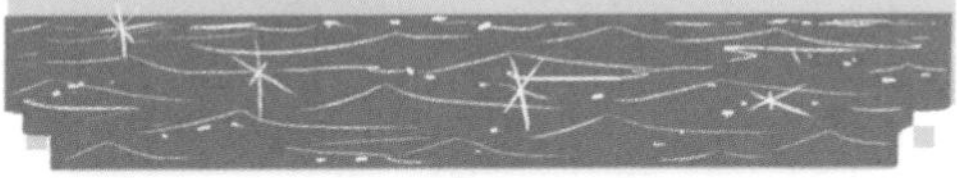

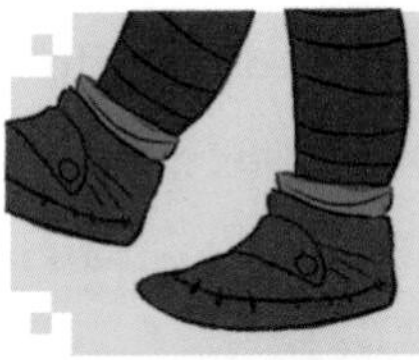

Legg
Leg

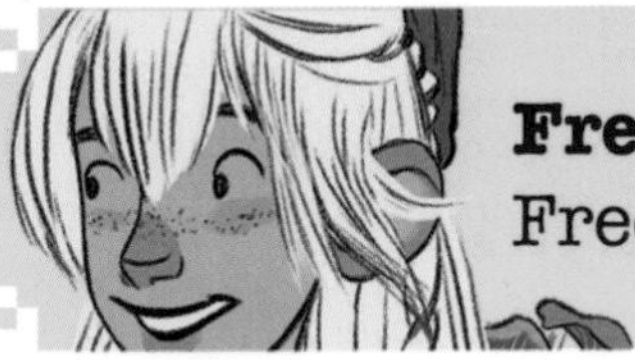

Frecknur
Freckles

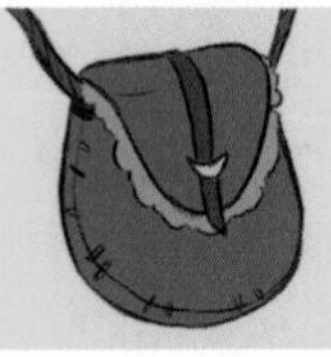

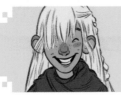

Bagg
Bag

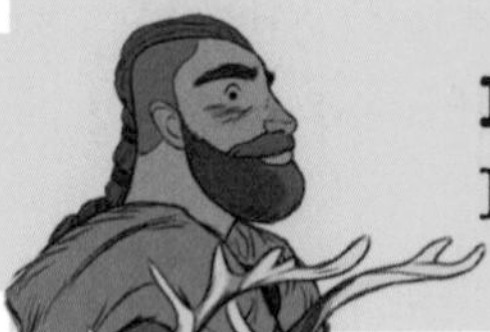

Húsbóndi
Husband

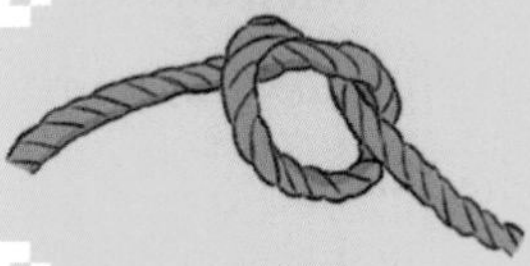

Knu
Knot

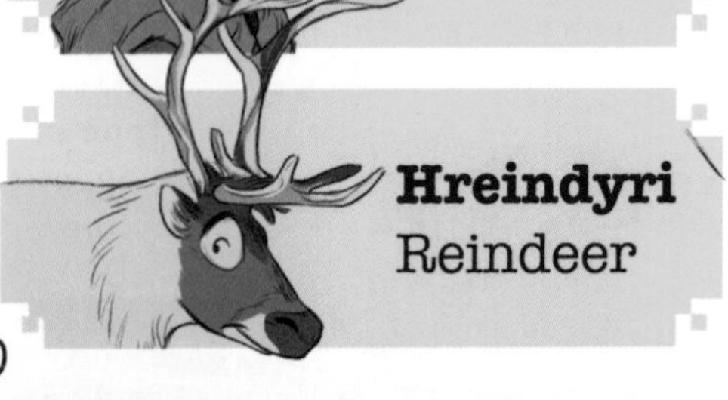

Hreindyri
Reindeer

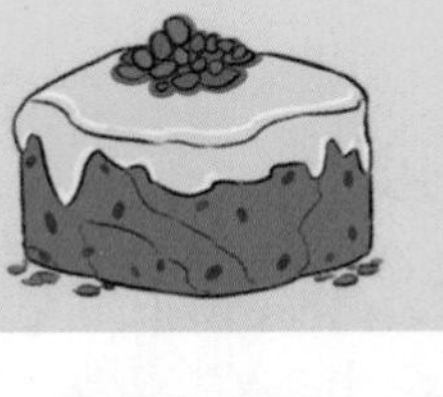

Kaka
Cake

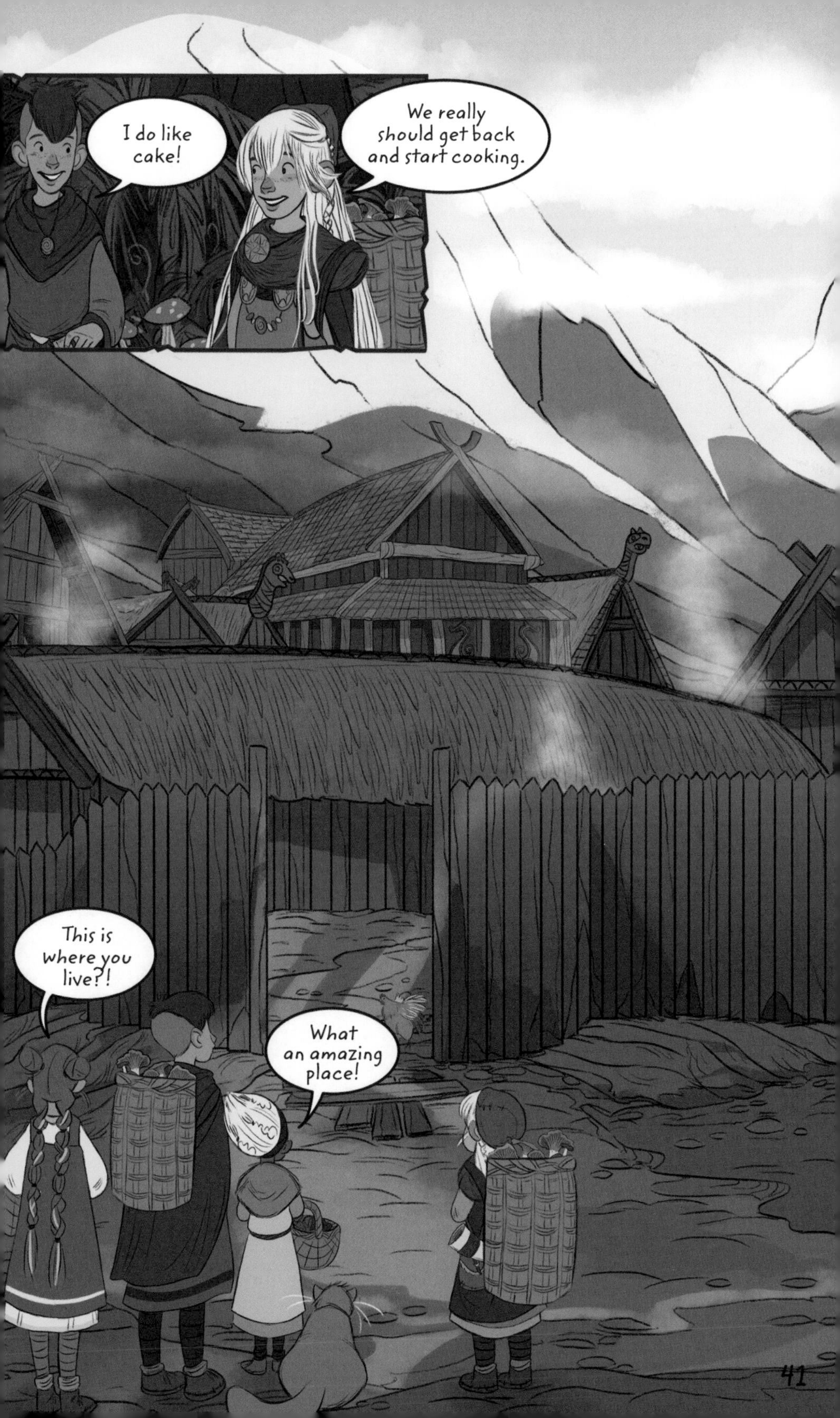

I do like cake!
We really should get back and start cooking.
This is where you live?!
What an amazing place!

Viking village

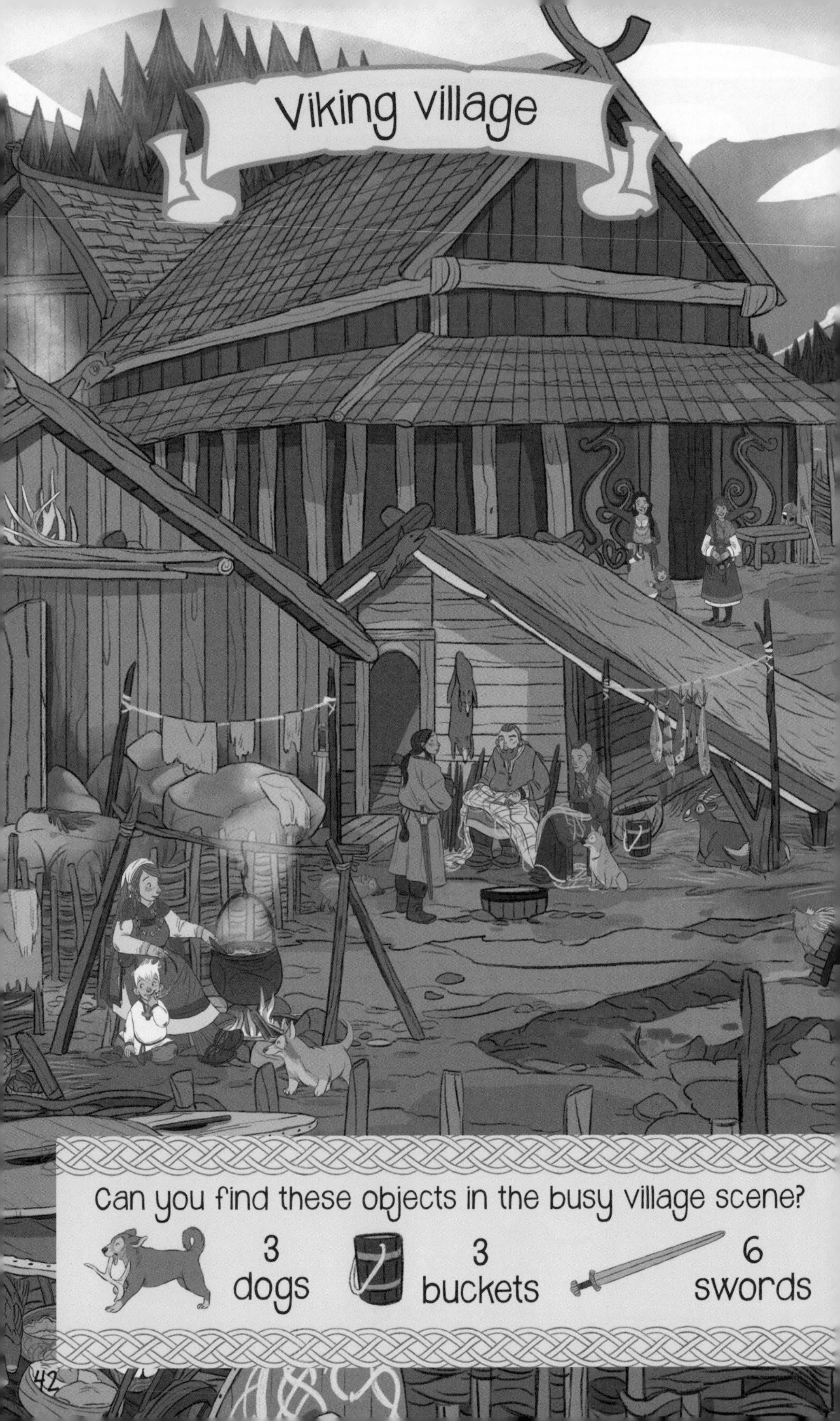

Can you find these objects in the busy village scene?

3 dogs

3 buckets

6 swords

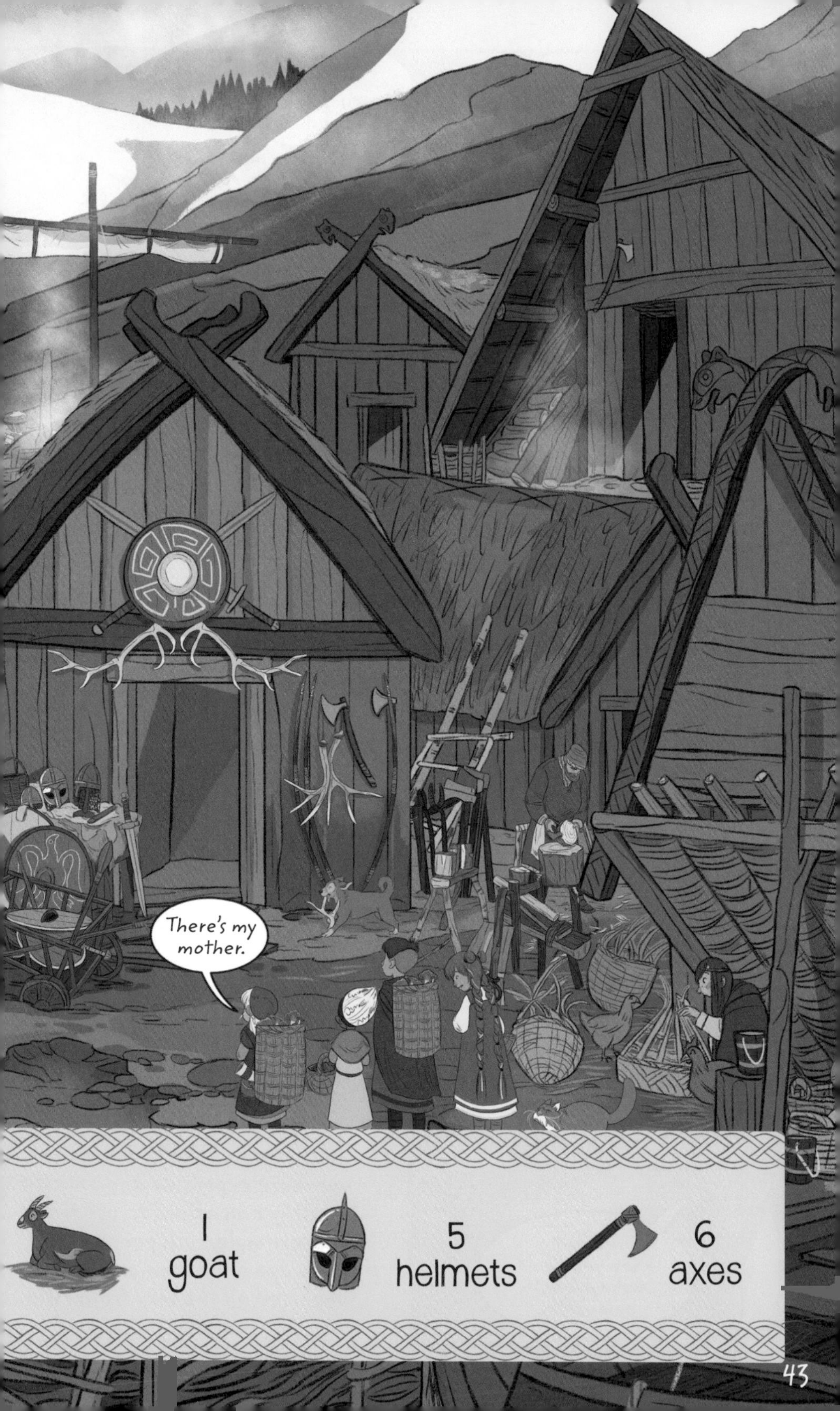
There's my mother.
1 goat
5 helmets
6 axes

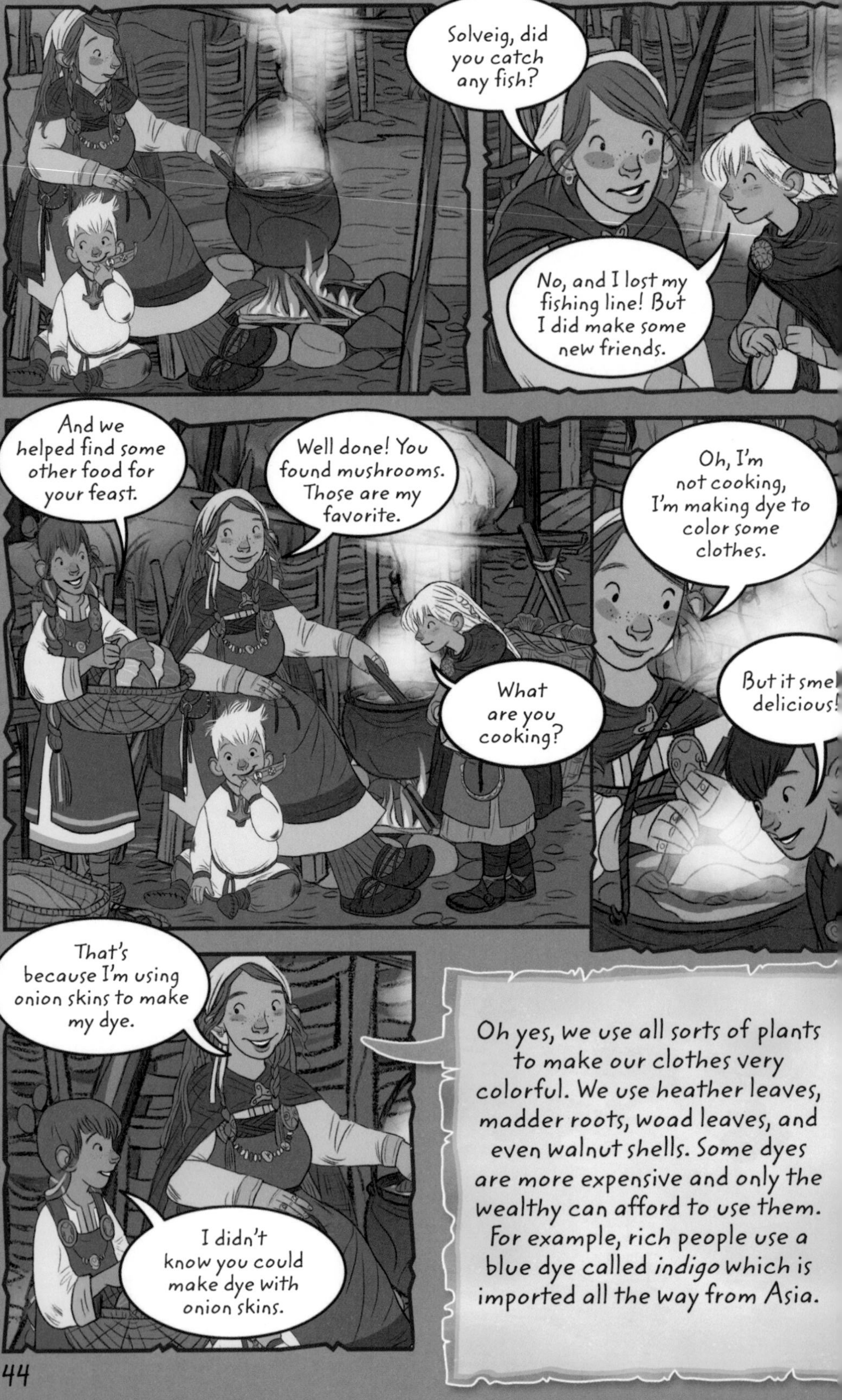
Solveig, did you catch any fish?
No, and I lost my fishing line! But I did make some new friends.
And we helped find some other food for your feast.
Well done! You found mushrooms. Those are my favorite.
What are you cooking?
Oh, I'm not cooking, I'm making dye to color some clothes.
But it sme delicious!
That's because I'm using onion skins to make my dye.
I didn't know you could make dye with onion skins.
Oh yes, we use all sorts of plants to make our clothes very colorful. We use heather leaves, madder roots, woad leaves, and even walnut shells. Some dyes are more expensive and only the wealthy can afford to use them. For example, rich people use a blue dye called *indigo* which is imported all the way from Asia.

Dye your own t-shirt

You will need:

- A large pot
- Some red or yellow onion skins
  (The more that you use, the stronger the dye will be.)
- A sieve
- 2 tablespoons of vinegar
- A white cotton t-shirt

1. Fill two thirds of the pot with water and add the onion skins.

2. Bring the water to a boil (make sure that an adult helps you with this) and cook the onion skins.

3. After about 20 minutes, use the sieve to take the onion skins out of the brightly colored water. Add the vinegar.

4. Put your t-shirt into the dye. Make sure that it is completely covered and leave it to soak overnight.

5. When you take the t-shirt out of the dye, rinse it in cold water and hang it up to dry.

The more onion skins you use, or the longer you soak your t-shirt, the brighter the color will be.

ike your dress!

Thank you very much. I like yours too.

Your cloak looks very warm!

It is. My cloak is made of wool but my dress is made of flax.

What's that?

Flax is a type of plant. We take fibers from the stem and weave them together to make fabric.

How clever!

Viking clothing

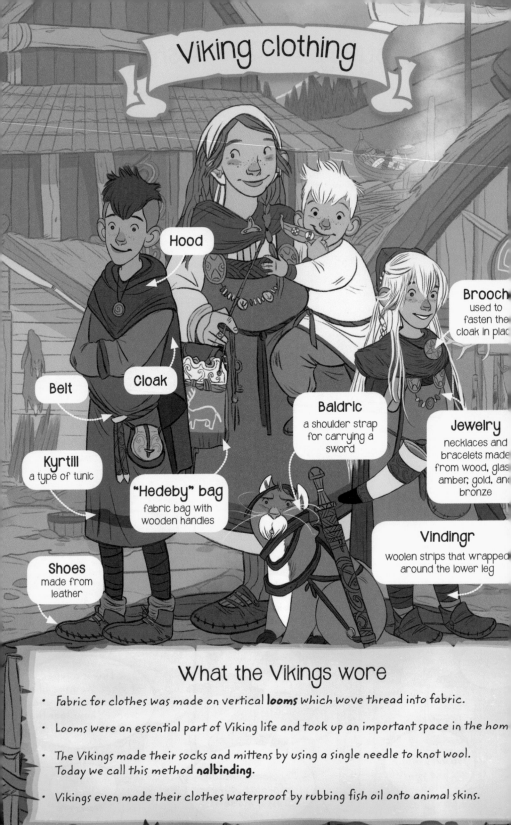

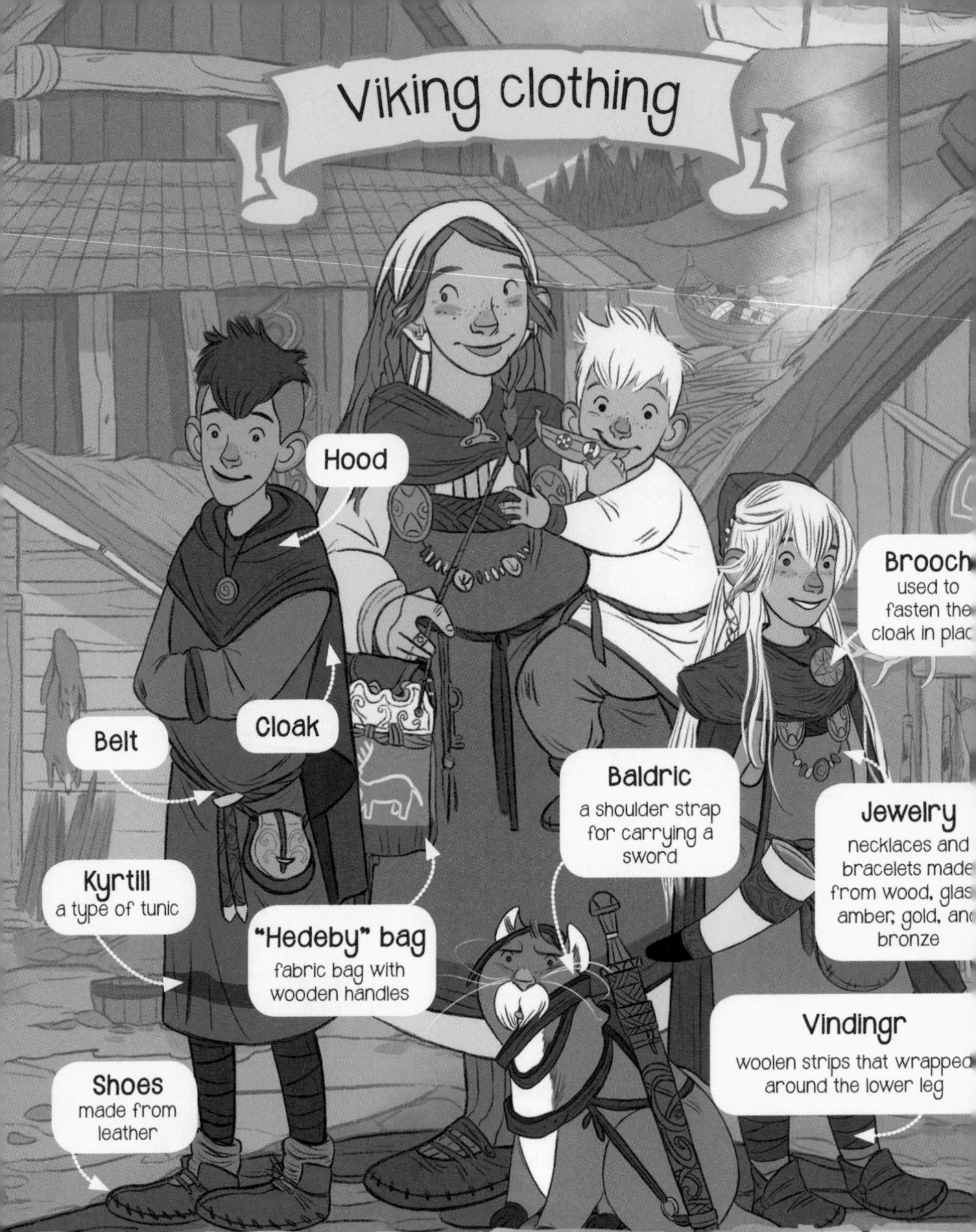
Hood
Cloak
Belt
Kyrtill
a type of tunic
"Hedeby" bag
fabric bag with wooden handles
Shoes
made from leather
Baldric
a shoulder strap for carrying a sword
Brooch
used to fasten the cloak in plac
Jewelry
necklaces and bracelets made from wood, glas amber, gold, an bronze
Vindingr
woolen strips that wrappe around the lower leg

What the Vikings wore

- Fabric for clothes was made on vertical **looms** which wove thread into fabric.
- Looms were an essential part of Viking life and took up an important space in the hom
- The Vikings made their socks and mittens by using a single needle to knot wool. Today we call this method **nalbinding**.
- Vikings even made their clothes waterproof by rubbing fish oil onto animal skins.

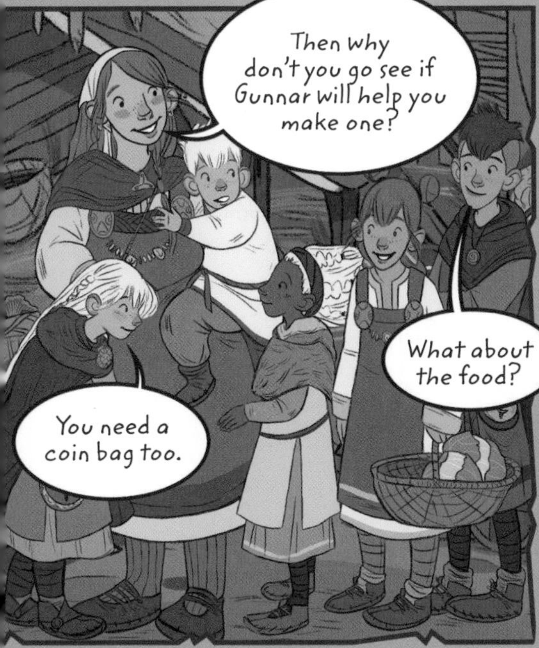
Then why don't you go see if Gunnar will help you make one?
What about the food?
You need a coin bag too.
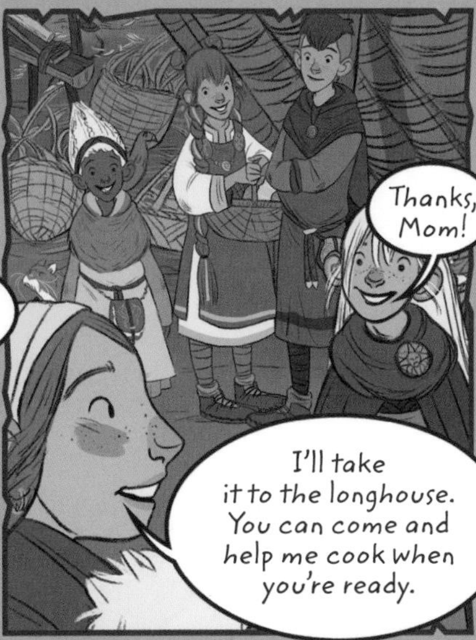
Thanks, Mom!
I'll take it to the longhouse. You can come and help me cook when you're ready.
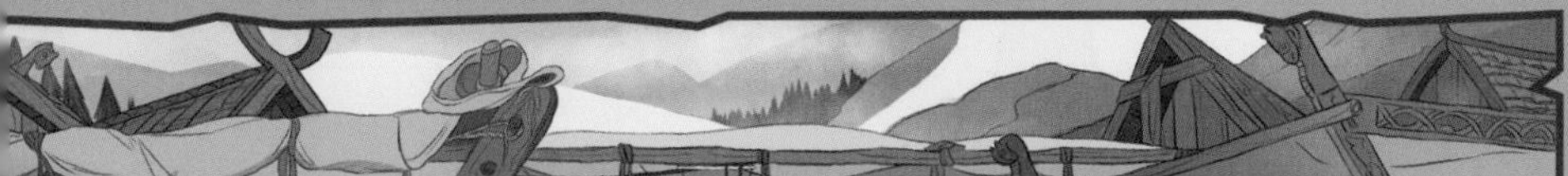

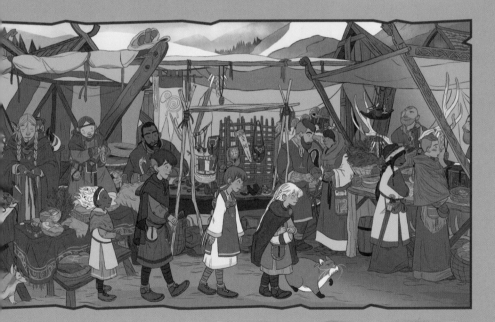

Crafts and trades

- Viking villages contained lots of different craftspeople.
- Everything that people needed to live or trade was made in the village.
- Craftspeople trained apprentices so that their skills were passed on.

Hi, Gunnar. Can you please show us how to make a purse?

Of course I can.

You will need:

- A small plate approximately 8 inches (20 cm) in diameter
- Fabric
  (You can use any kind. The Vikings would have used leather but we like felt.)
- A ruler
- A pen
- Scissors
- A shoelace

1. Place the plate onto the fabric. Draw around it and cut out the circle.

2. Measure and cut a series of holes about 0.5 inches (1.0 cm) from the top edge of the circle. The holes don't have to be neat but there should be an even number of them.

3. Thread the shoelace in and out of the holes you have made.

4. Tie the ends of the shoelace together and gather up the top of the circle to make your pouch.

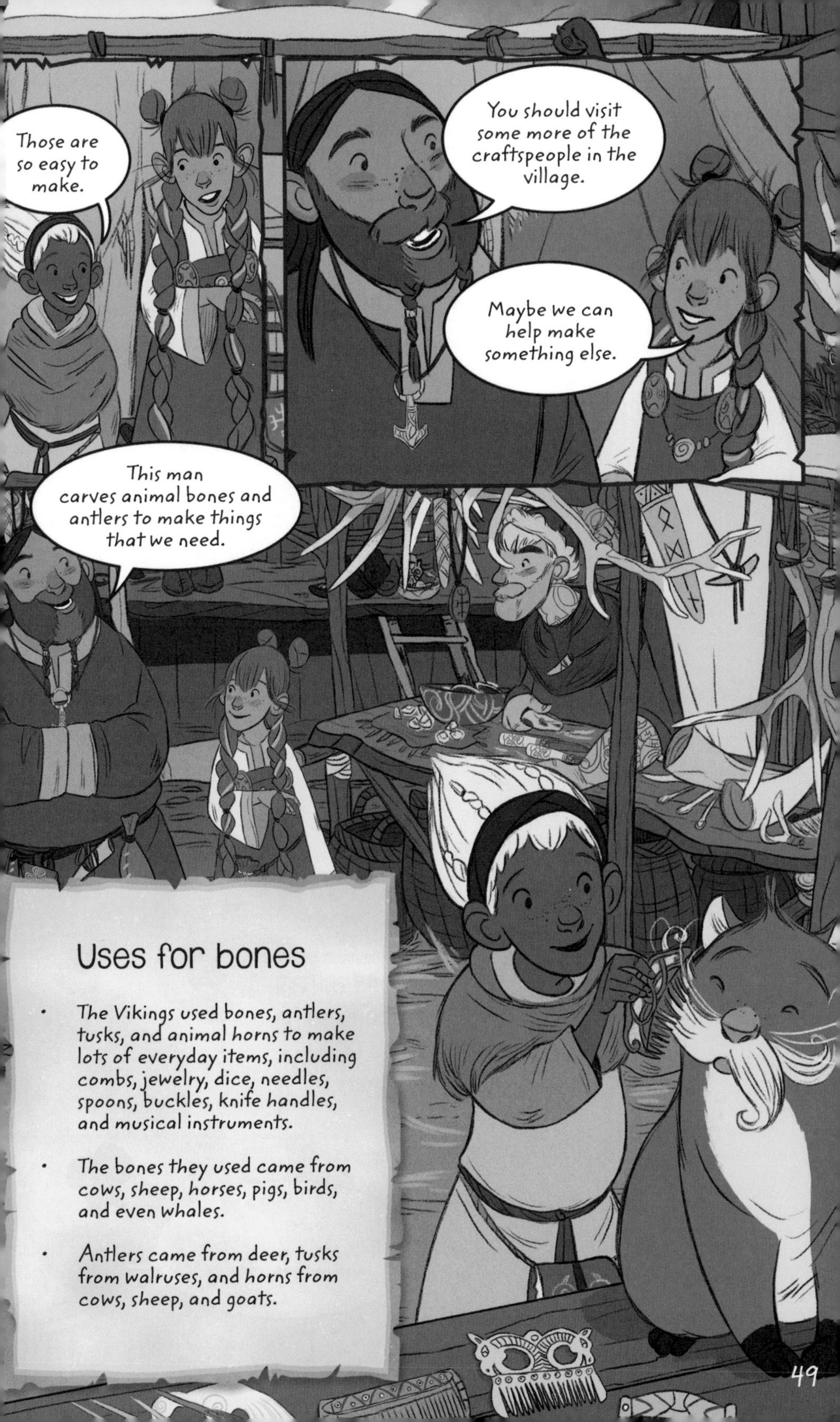
Those are so easy to make.
You should visit some more of the craftspeople in the village.
Maybe we can help make something else.
This man carves animal bones and antlers to make things that we need.

Uses for bones

- The Vikings used bones, antlers, tusks, and animal horns to make lots of everyday items, including combs, jewelry, dice, needles, spoons, buckles, knife handles, and musical instruments.
- The bones they used came from cows, sheep, horses, pigs, birds, and even whales.
- Antlers came from deer, tusks from walruses, and horns from cows, sheep, and goats.

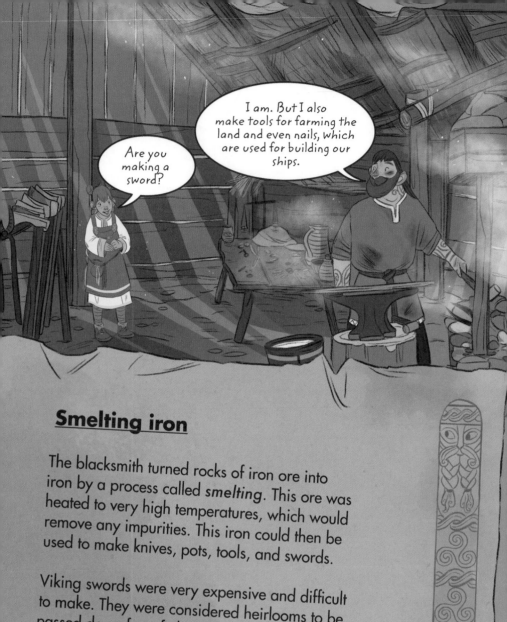

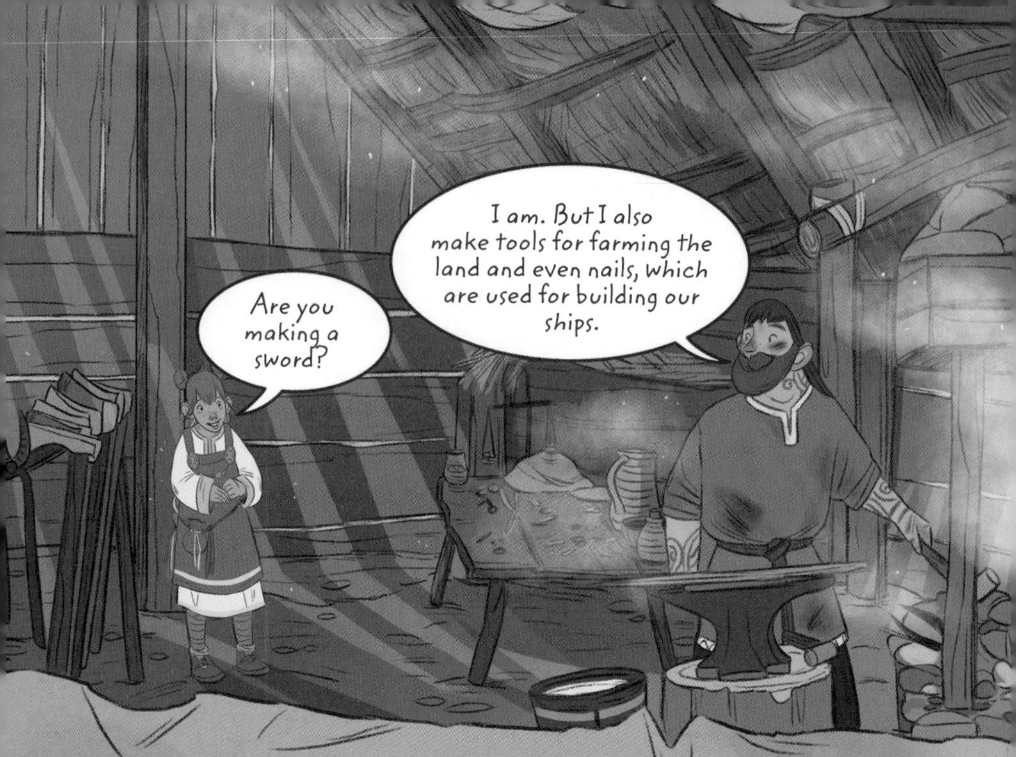
Are you making a sword?
I am. But I also make tools for farming the land and even nails, which are used for building our ships.

Smelting iron

The blacksmith turned rocks of iron ore into iron by a process called *smelting*. This ore was heated to very high temperatures, which would remove any impurities. This iron could then be used to make knives, pots, tools, and swords.

Viking swords were very expensive and difficult to make. They were considered heirlooms to be passed down from father to son. Some of these swords were given names by their owners, such as Leg-biter, War Flame, Peace-breaker, and Villain.

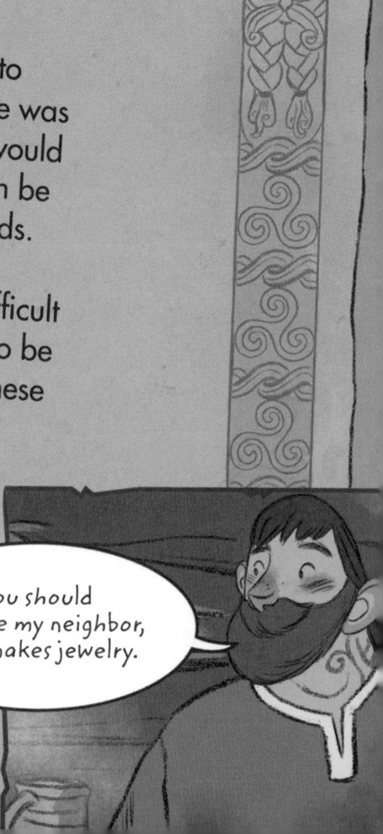
You should also see my neighbor, who makes jewelry.

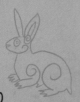

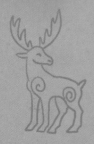

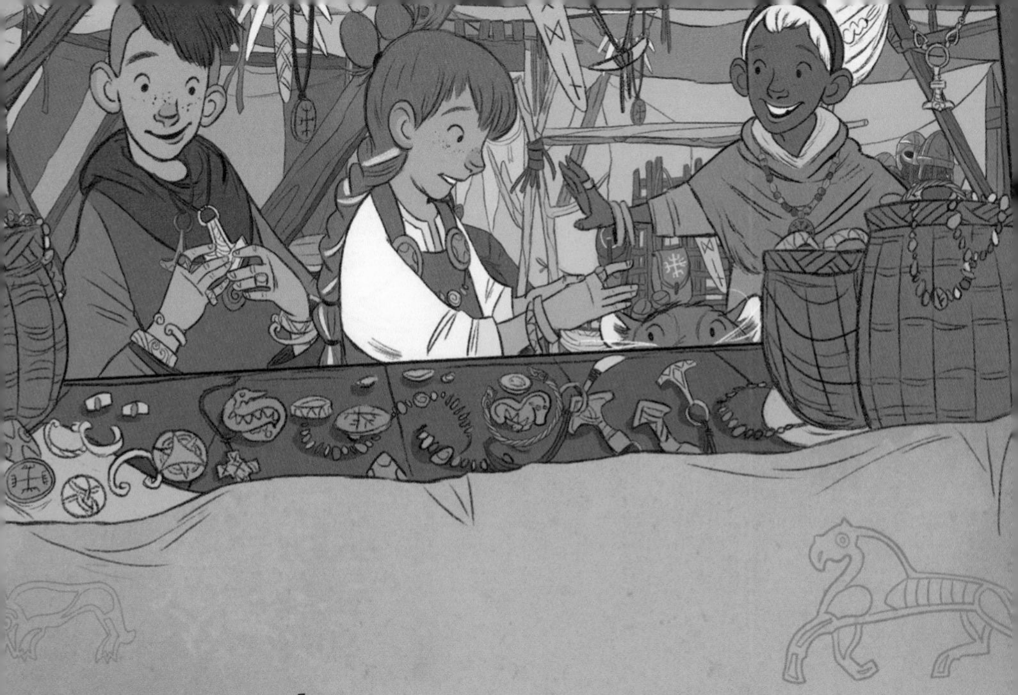

Jewelry

Both Viking men and women wore jewelry as a sign of their wealth. Gold was very rare and so most Viking jewelry was made of silver or bronze. Some jewelry could be broken up to pay for things. This was called *hacksilver*. Jewelry was also made of glass and amber beads.

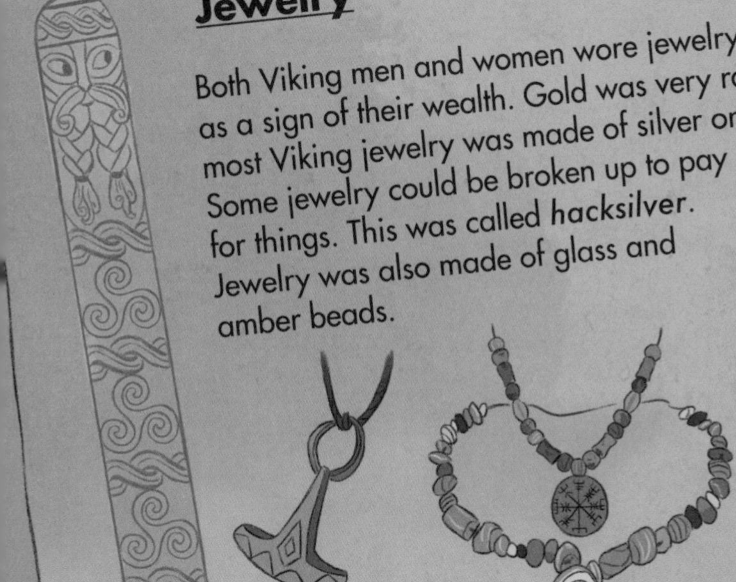

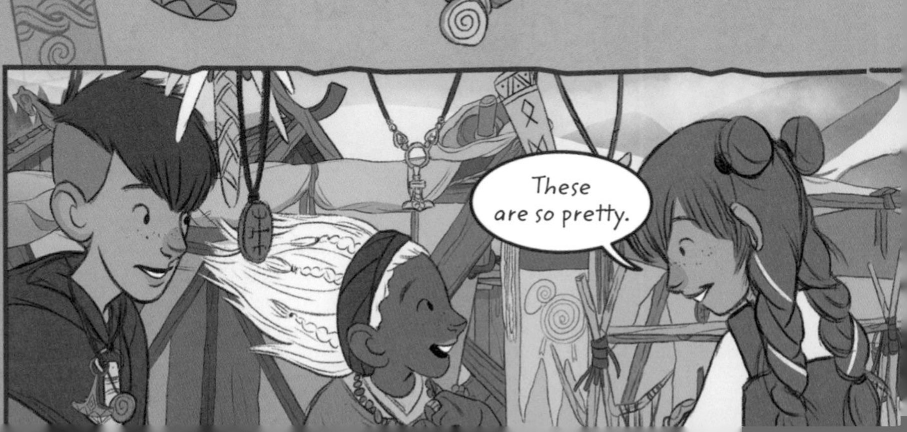
These are so pretty.

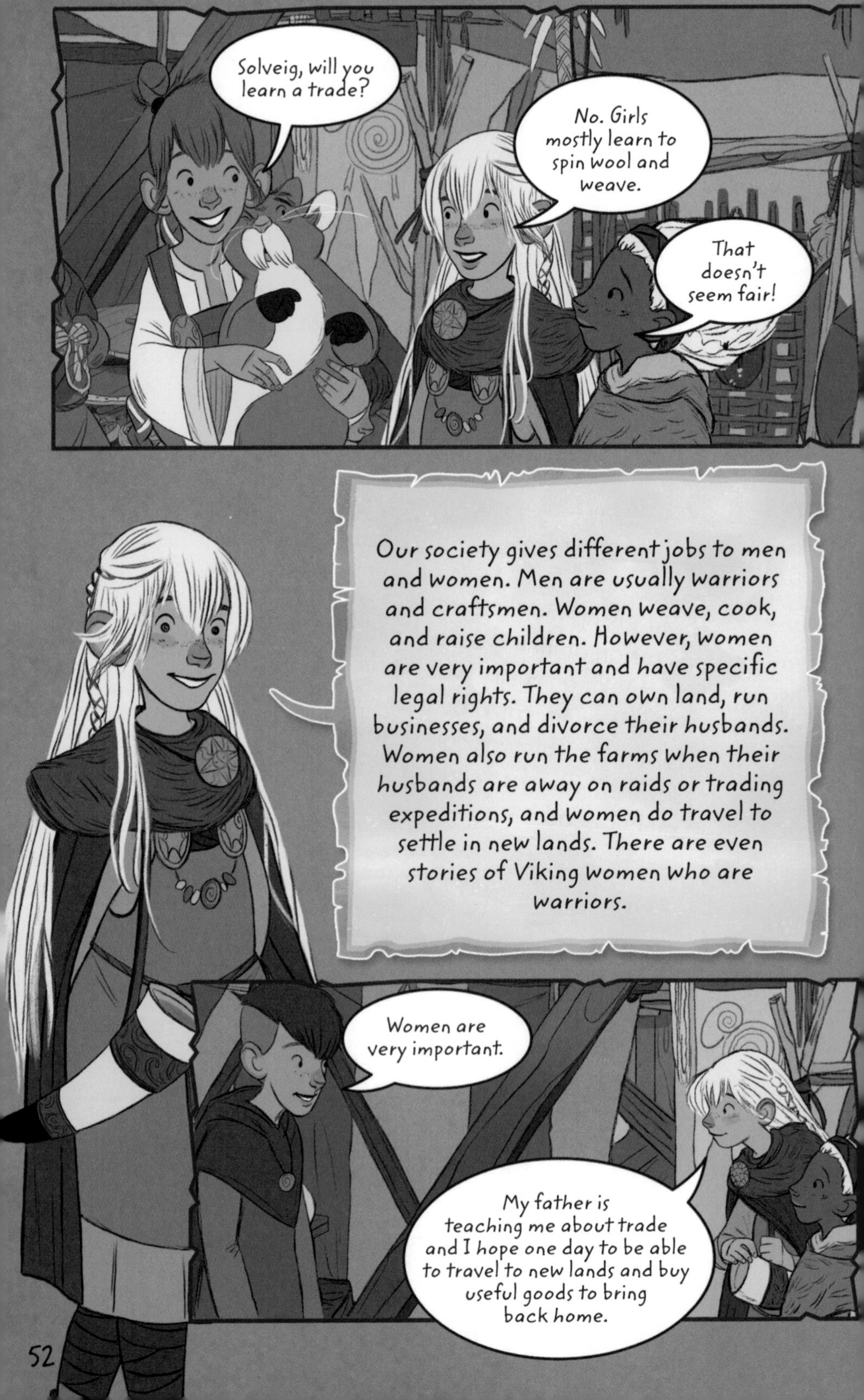
Solveig, will you learn a trade?
No. Girls mostly learn to spin wool and weave.
That doesn't seem fair!
Our society gives different jobs to men and women. Men are usually warriors and craftsmen. Women weave, cook, and raise children. However, women are very important and have specific legal rights. They can own land, run businesses, and divorce their husbands. Women also run the farms when their husbands are away on raids or trading expeditions, and women do travel to settle in new lands. There are even stories of Viking women who are warriors.
Women are very important.
My father is teaching me about trade and I hope one day to be able to travel to new lands and buy useful goods to bring back home.

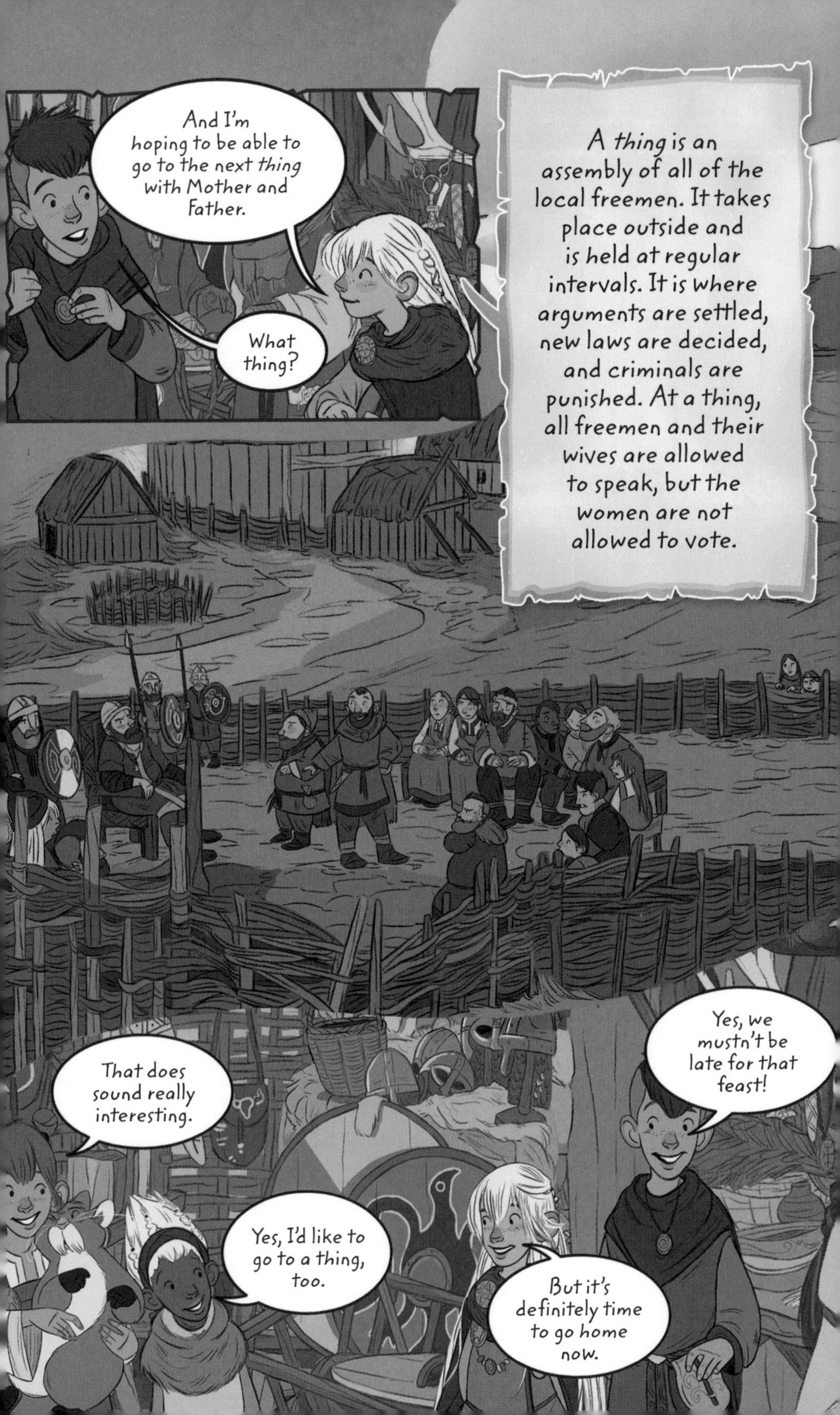
And I'm hoping to be able to go to the next *thing* with Mother and Father.
What thing?
A *thing* is an assembly of all of the local freemen. It takes place outside and is held at regular intervals. It is where arguments are settled, new laws are decided, and criminals are punished. At a thing, all freemen and their wives are allowed to speak, but the women are not allowed to vote.
That does sound really interesting.
Yes, I'd like to go to a thing, too.
But it's definitely time to go home now.
Yes, we mustn't be late for that feast!

Inside the longhouse

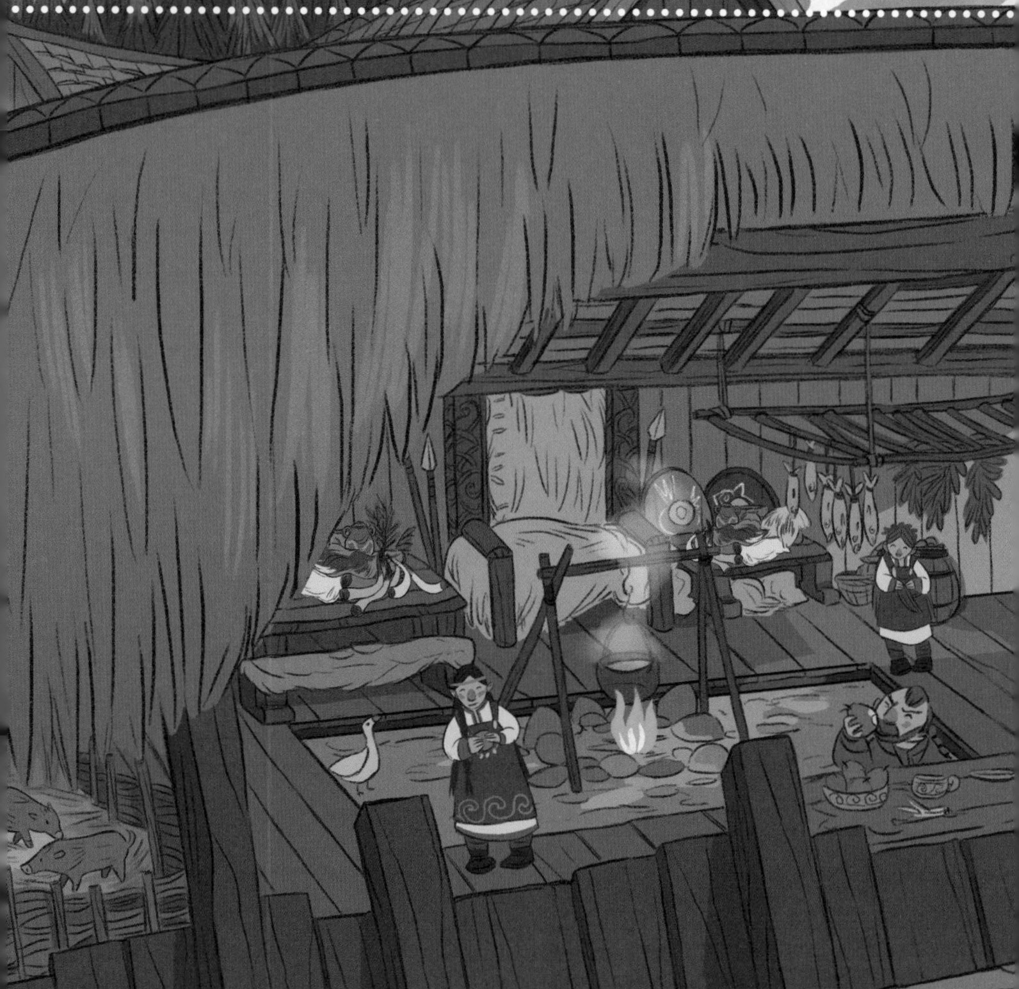

Viking longhouses

- Many Vikings lived inside long, narrow houses called **langhús**, or longhouses.
- Longhouses were built of wood, which was covered in peat, **daub**, and **wattle**.
- Daub is made up of mud, straw, and manure, which is then packed on top of a framework of wooden strips, called wattle, and left to dry.
- At their widest points, the walls of a longhouse could be 5 feet (1.5 m) thick.
- The largest known Viking longhouse that archaeologists have uncovered is 272 feet (83 m) long.

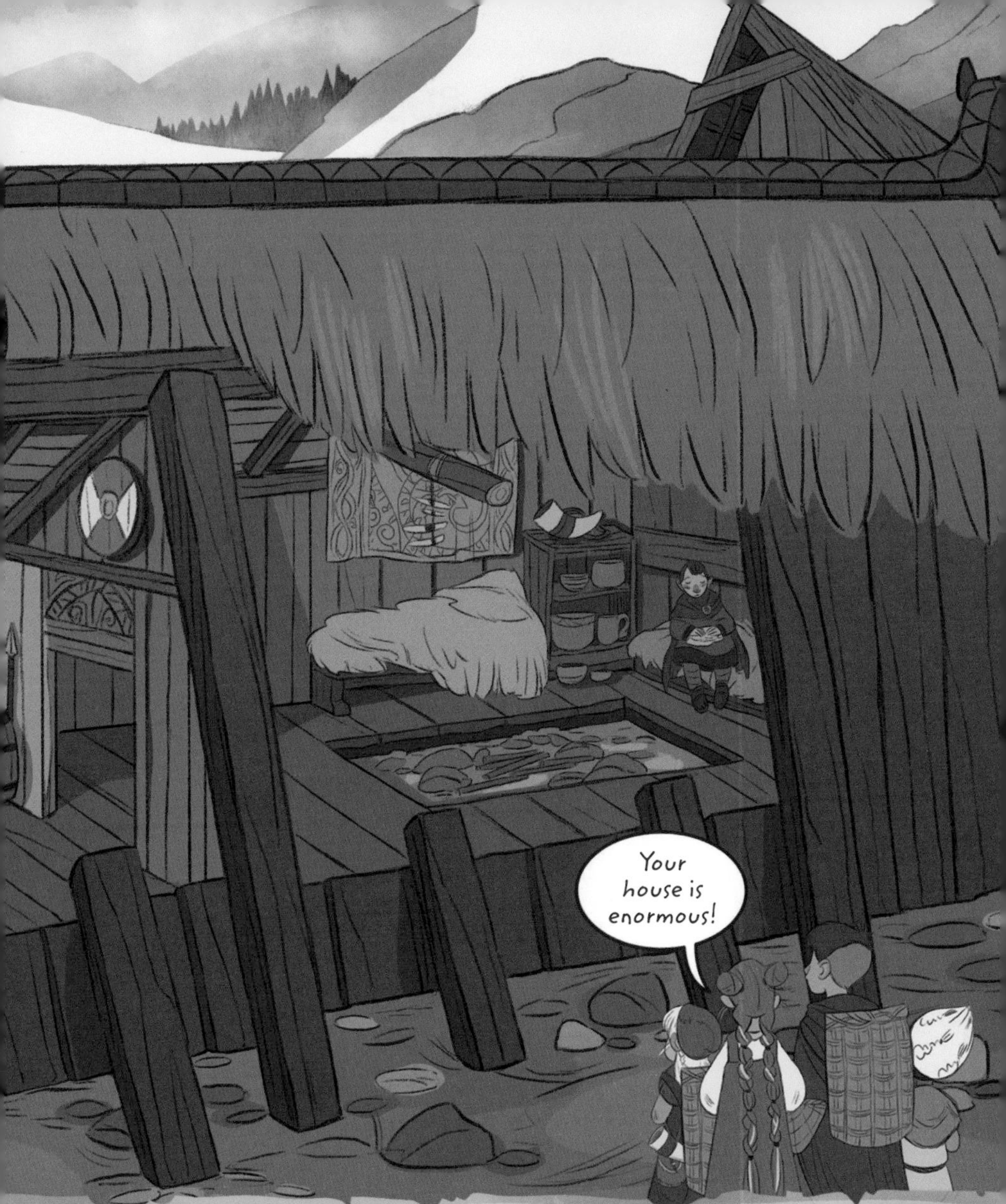
Your house is enormous!

Living in a longhouse

- Longhouses were divided into different living spaces, and many families lived in the same building.
- Fires were built indoors. The smoke escaped through holes in the roof.
- Longhouses had no windows, so the only light that came in was from the front door, the smoke holes in the roof, or oil lamps.
- Benches were placed along the outer edges of the longhouse for people to sit or sleep on. Beds were very unusual, and most Vikings slept sitting on benches.

A Viking appetite

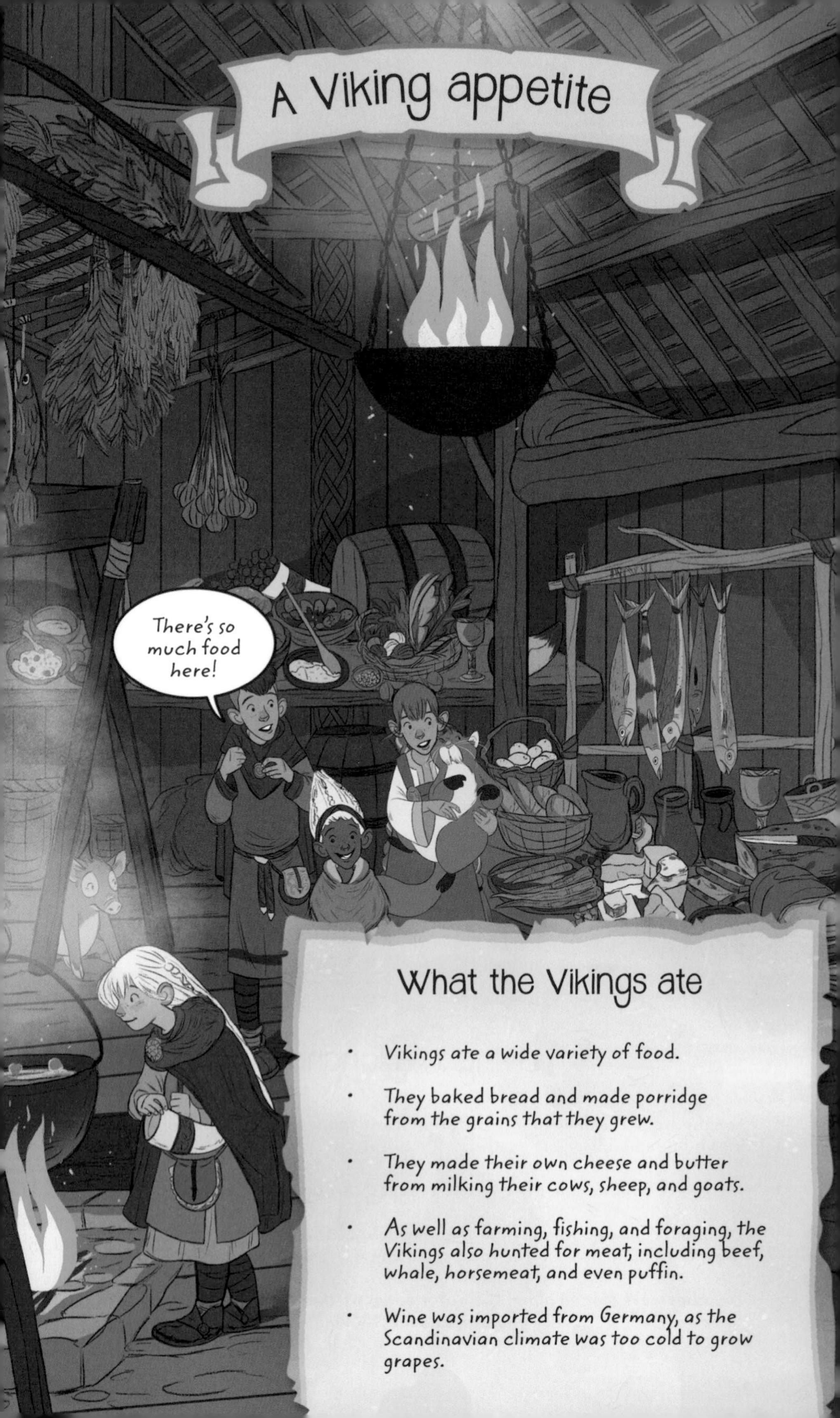
There's so much food here!

What the Vikings ate

- Vikings ate a wide variety of food.
- They baked bread and made porridge from the grains that they grew.
- They made their own cheese and butter from milking their cows, sheep, and goats.
- As well as farming, fishing, and foraging, the Vikings also hunted for meat, including beef, whale, horsemeat, and even puffin.
- Wine was imported from Germany, as the Scandinavian climate was too cold to grow grapes.

Preserving food

- Vikings didn't have refrigerators, so they used different methods to preserve their food and make it last through the winter.
- Some vegetables and meats could be pickled in vinegar, salt, or whey.
- Whey is the liquid that is left over after milk has been curdled to make cheese.
- Meat, fish, vegetables, grain, and fruit could all be dried, and lots of meats could also be smoked to make them last longer.
- In areas where the Vikings had access to salt, they could use salt to preserve cheese, fish, and fatty meats.
- Fermentation was used to preserve meat, vegetables, and cheese by using acids that come from bacteria.

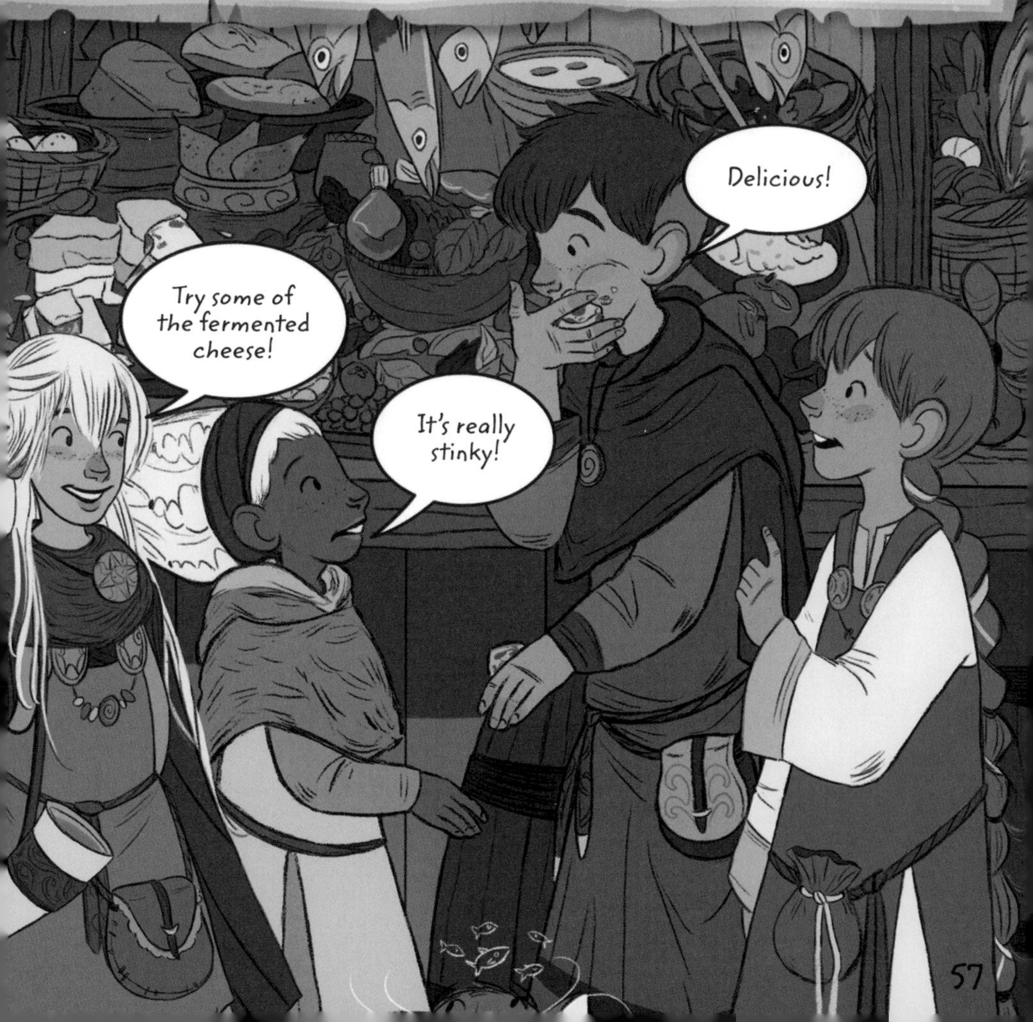
Delicious!
Try some of the fermented cheese!
It's really stinky!

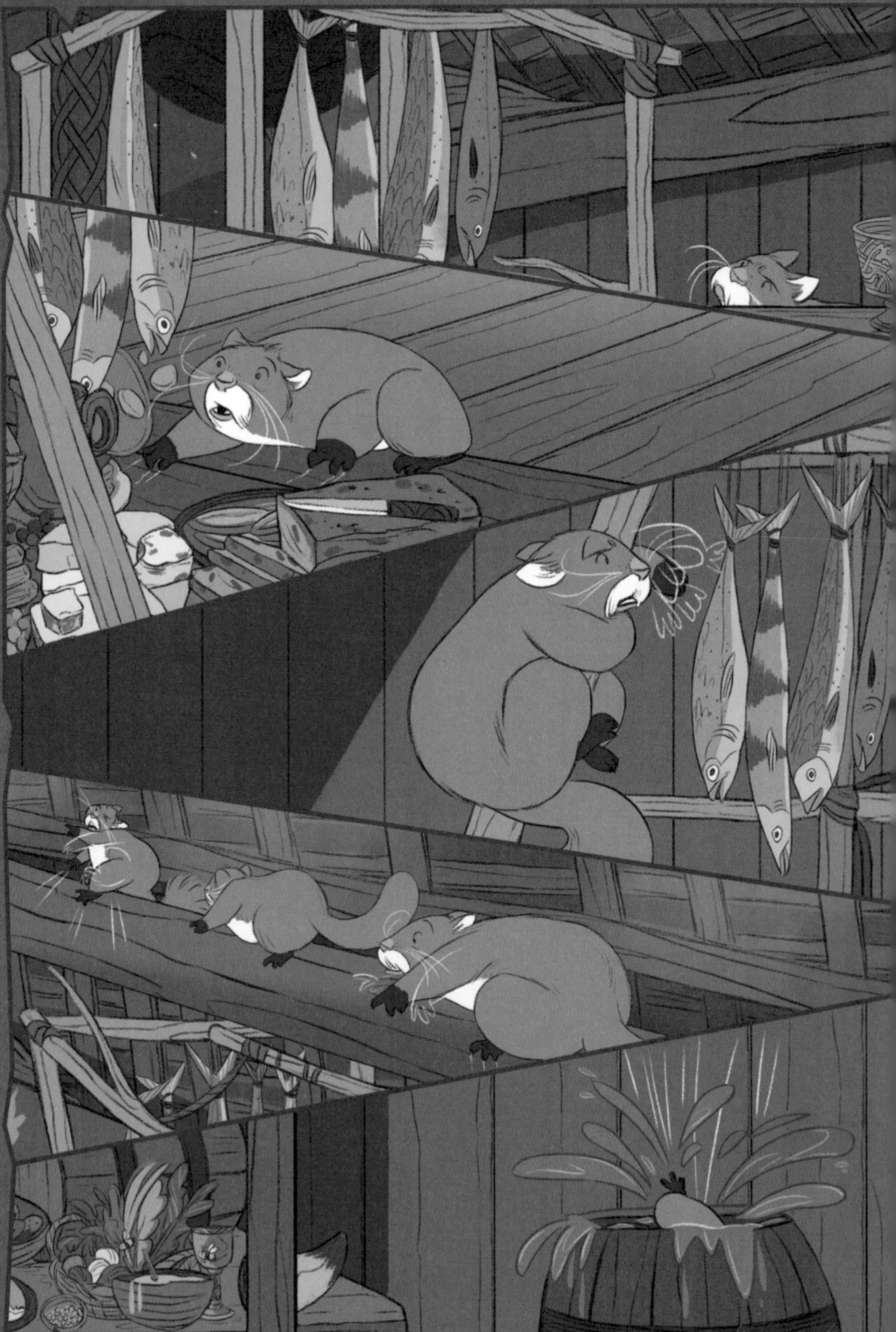

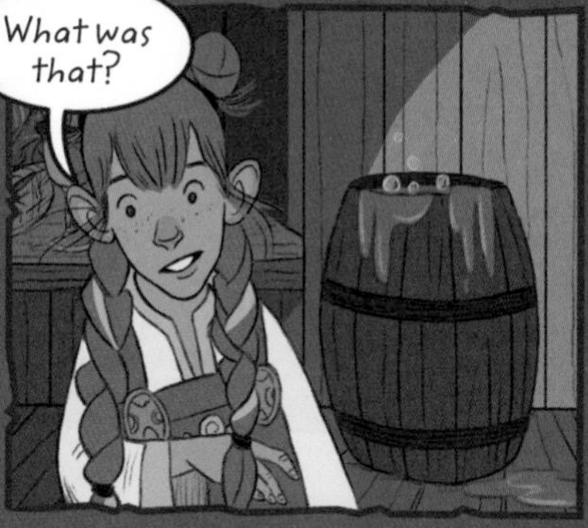
What was that?

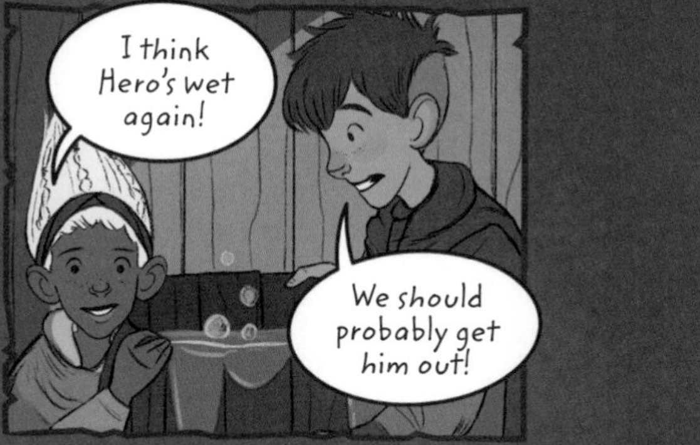
I think Hero's wet again!
We should probably get him out!

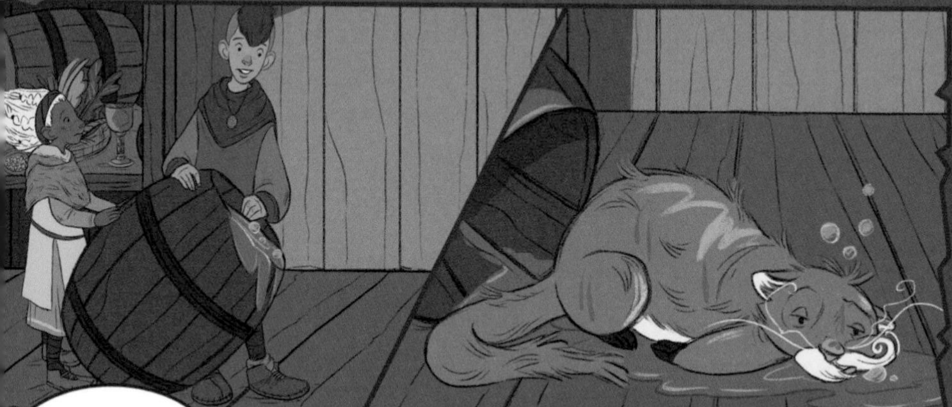

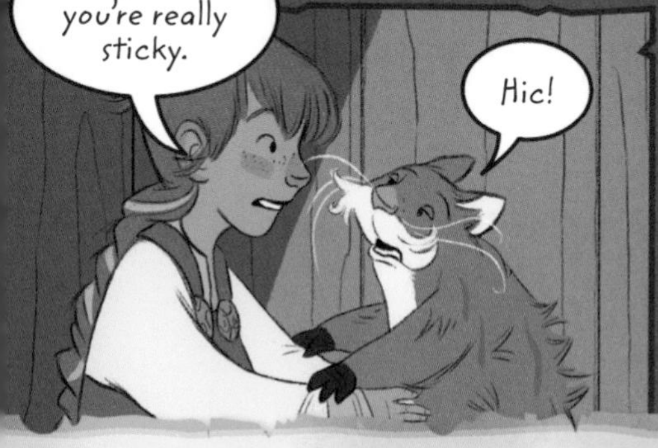
Oh, Hero, you're really sticky.
Hic!

Drinking

The Vikings brewed their own beer and ale, which were made by fermenting grains.

Herbs were added to drinks to give them different flavors.

Mead was an alcoholic drink that was made from honey.

Even children drank ale every day!

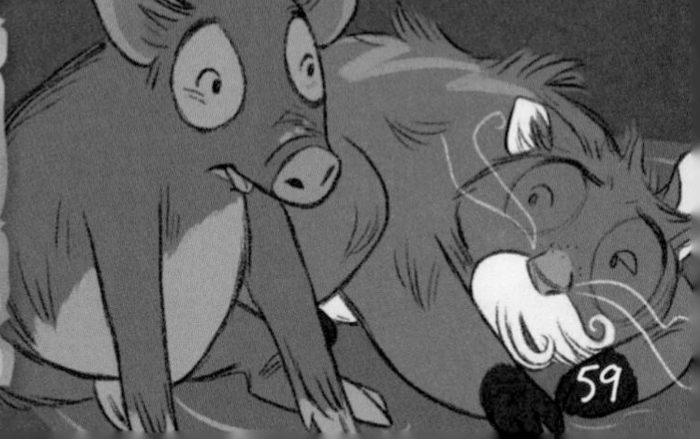

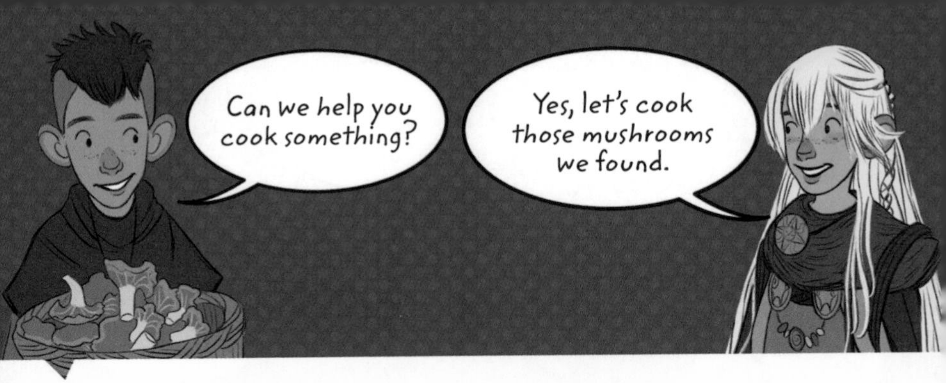
Can we help you cook something?
Yes, let's cook those mushrooms we found.

Recipe for mushroom soup

Always wash your hands before cooking and make sure you get an adult to help you use the stove.

Ingredients:
2 tablespoons of butter
1 large onion, finely chopped
2 cloves of garlic, crushed
2 sticks of celery, finely chopped
8.5 cups (600 g) of mushrooms, finely chopped (You can use whichever ones you like, but the Vikings ate a kind that we call chanterelles.)
1 cup (250 mL) of vegetable stock
1 cup (250 mL) of semi-skimmed milk
Salt and pepper

Melt the butter in a pan.
Add the onion and garlic and cook until soft.
Stir in the mushrooms and celery until all of the vegetables are soft.
Pour in the vegetable stock and milk and stir for around 20 minutes, until the soup is steaming hot.
Add salt and pepper to taste.

Enjoy!

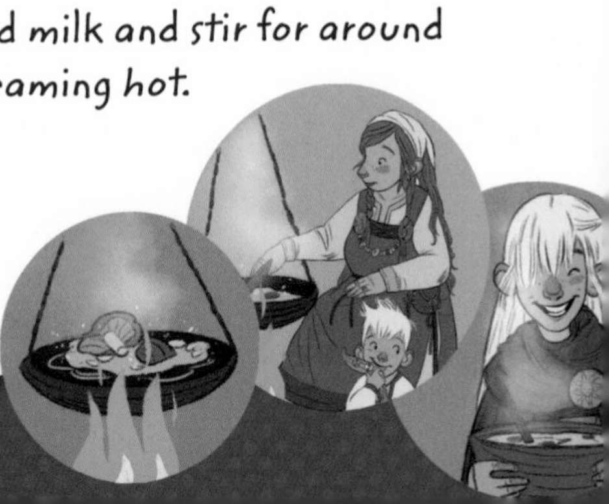

Make non-alcoholic mead

Ingredients:

3/4 cups (250 g) of honey
1/2 cup (125 ml) of apple juice
1.5 cups (375 ml) of water
Spices (You can experiment with your favorites — the Vikings liked fennel seeds.)

Place all of the ingredients into a pan and bring them to a boil.
Keep stirring them and let the mixture simmer for around 30 minutes.
Leave the liquid to cool.
Carefully pour your delicious mead into a jug through a sieve to take out the bits of spices.
Place the jug in the fridge until you are ready for a delicious, sweet drink.

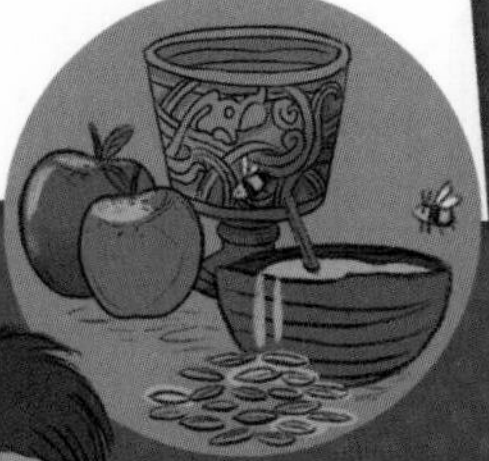

At the table

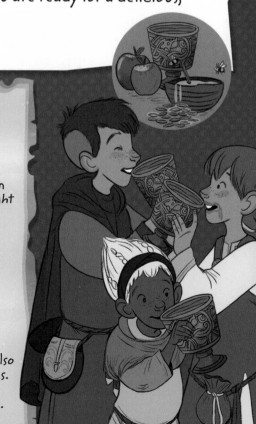

The Vikings ate two meals each day.

Dagverðr, meaning day meal, was eaten in the mid-morning. **Náttverðr**, meaning night meal, was eaten in the evening.

The Vikings usually sat at benches to eat.

Their plates and bowls were mostly made from wood and sometimes pottery.

Vikings ate with knives, but forks hadn't been invented yet.

Cups were made from wood but Vikings also drank out of brass bowls and animal horns.

Shells were used as ladles for serving food.

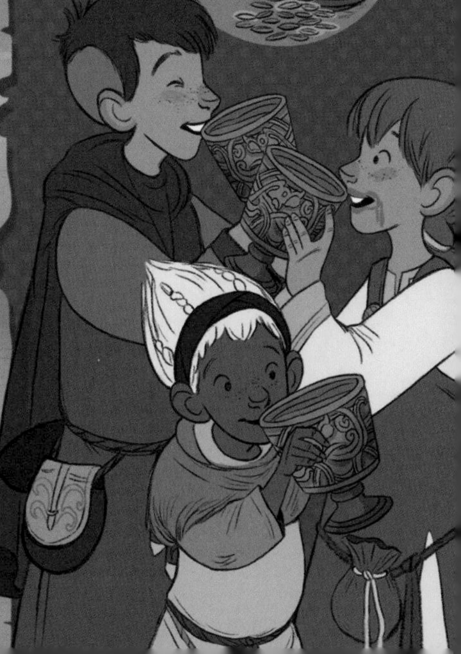

Weights, measurements, and values

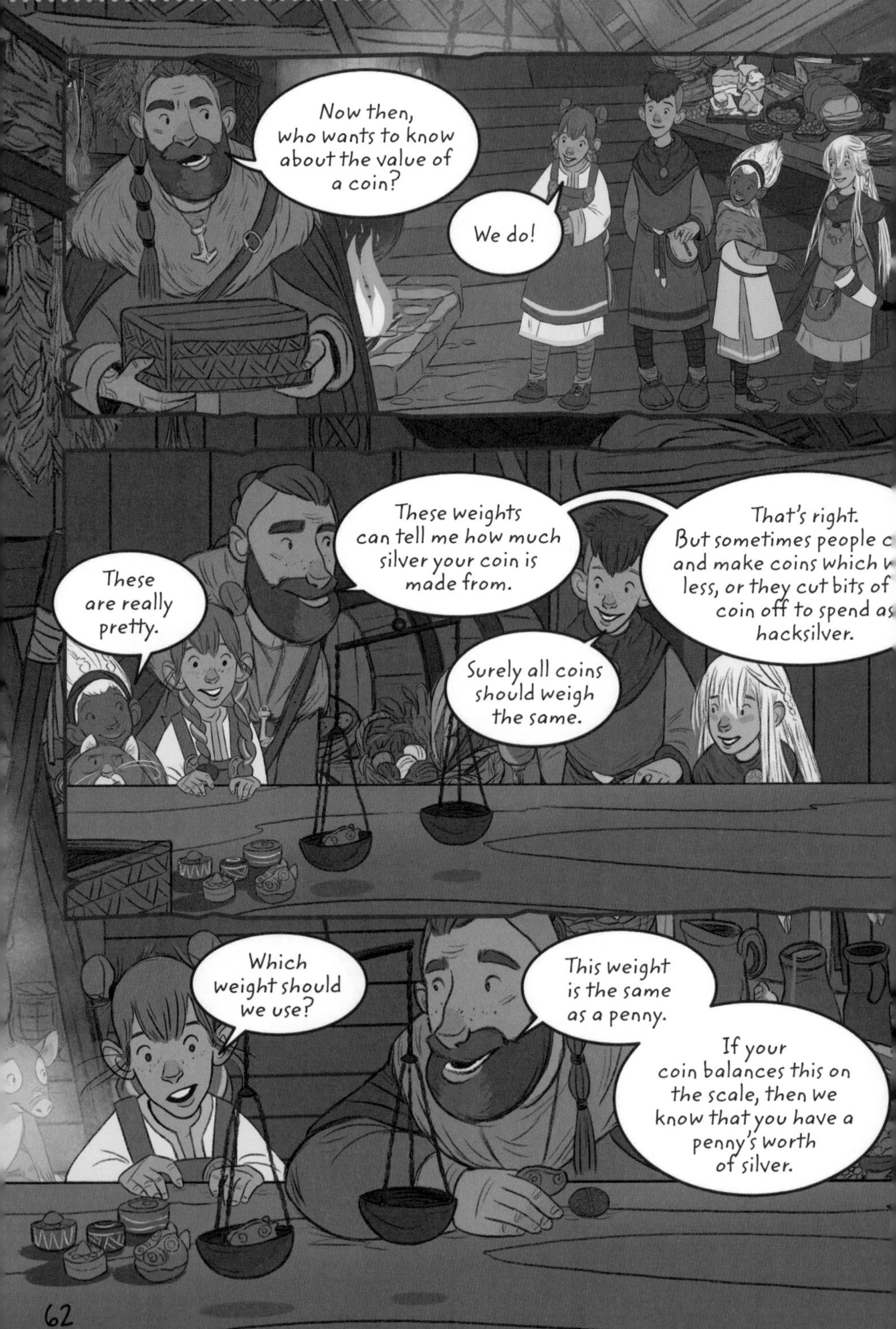

Now then, who wants to know about the value of a coin?
We do!
These are really pretty.
These weights can tell me how much silver your coin is made from.
Surely all coins should weigh the same.
That's right. But sometimes people c and make coins which w less, or they cut bits of coin off to spend as hacksilver.
Which weight should we use?
This weight is the same as a penny.
If your coin balances this on the scale, then we know that you have a penny's worth of silver.

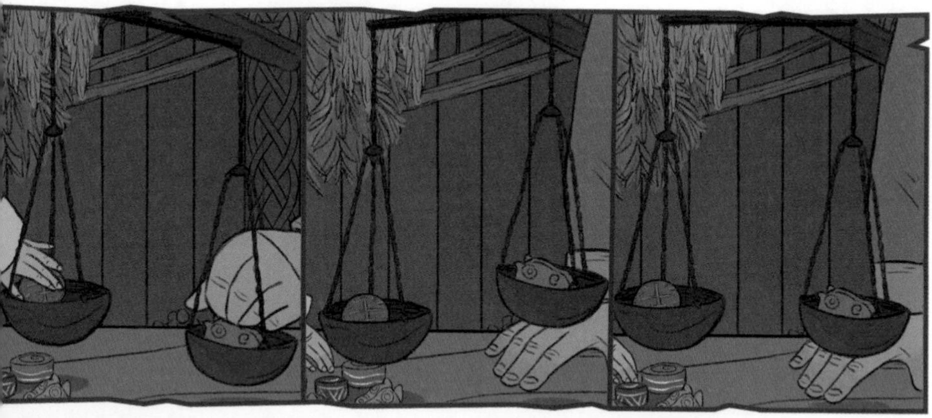

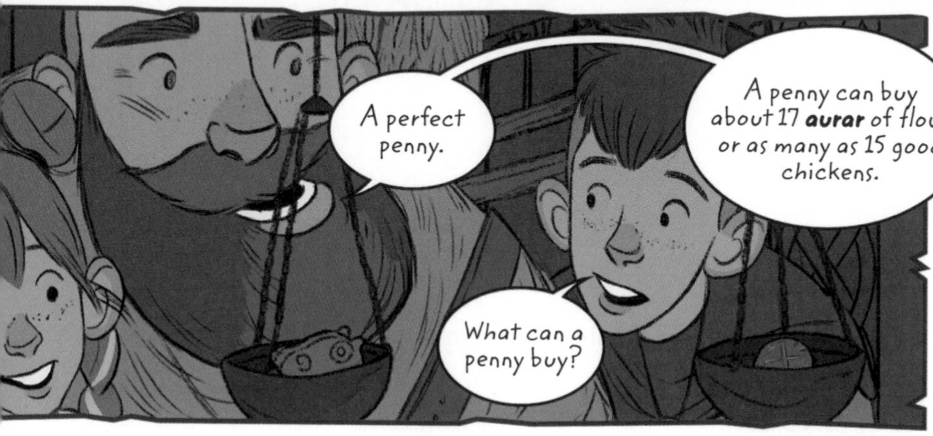

A perfect penny.
What can a penny buy?
A penny can buy about 17 **aurar** of flour or as many as 15 good chickens.

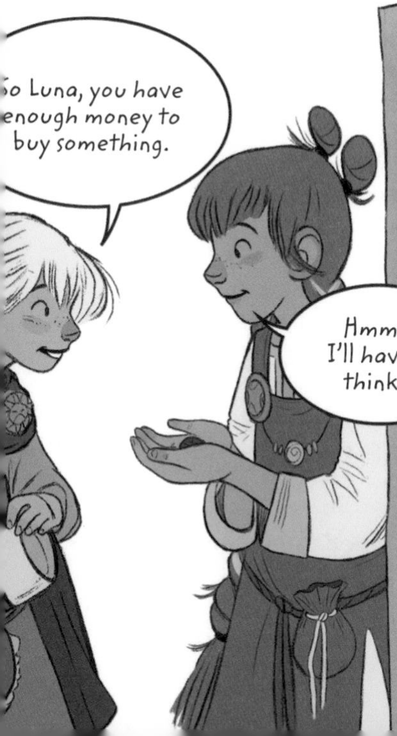

So Luna, you have enough money to buy something.
Hmmm, I'll have to think...

Viking weights

- An **eyrir** (plural *aurar*) is a measure that is roughly 1ounce (28 g) in weight.
- An **örtug** is 1/3 of an eyrir.
- A **mörk** (plural *merkur*) is the same as 8 aurar.
- A **pund** is worth 24 merkur.

Well, why don't we play a game while we wait for the food to cook?

What shall we play?

Let's play **Hnefatafl!**

How to play Hnefatafl

You will need:

Three different colored counters:

- 24 x Attackers
- 12 x Defenders
- 1 x King

How to play:

1. Set out the counters as shown with the King piece on the center square

2. Players take turns moving their pieces.

3. Each piece can move any number of spaces but only in a straight (not diagonal) line.

4. A piece is captured when it is surrounded by the opposite team on two sides, except for the King, which must be surrounded on all four sides by the Attackers.

5. When a piece is captured, it must be removed from the board.

6. The aim of the game is to get the King to safety on any one of the corner spaces without being captured by the attacking pieces.

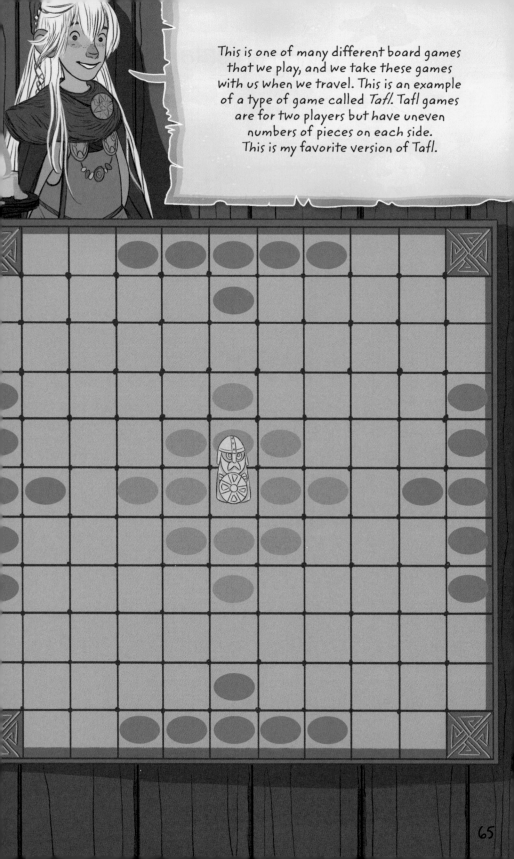

This is one of many different board games that we play, and we take these games with us when we travel. This is an example of a type of game called *Tafl*. Tafl games are for two players but have uneven numbers of pieces on each side. This is my favorite version of Tafl.

Viking entertainment

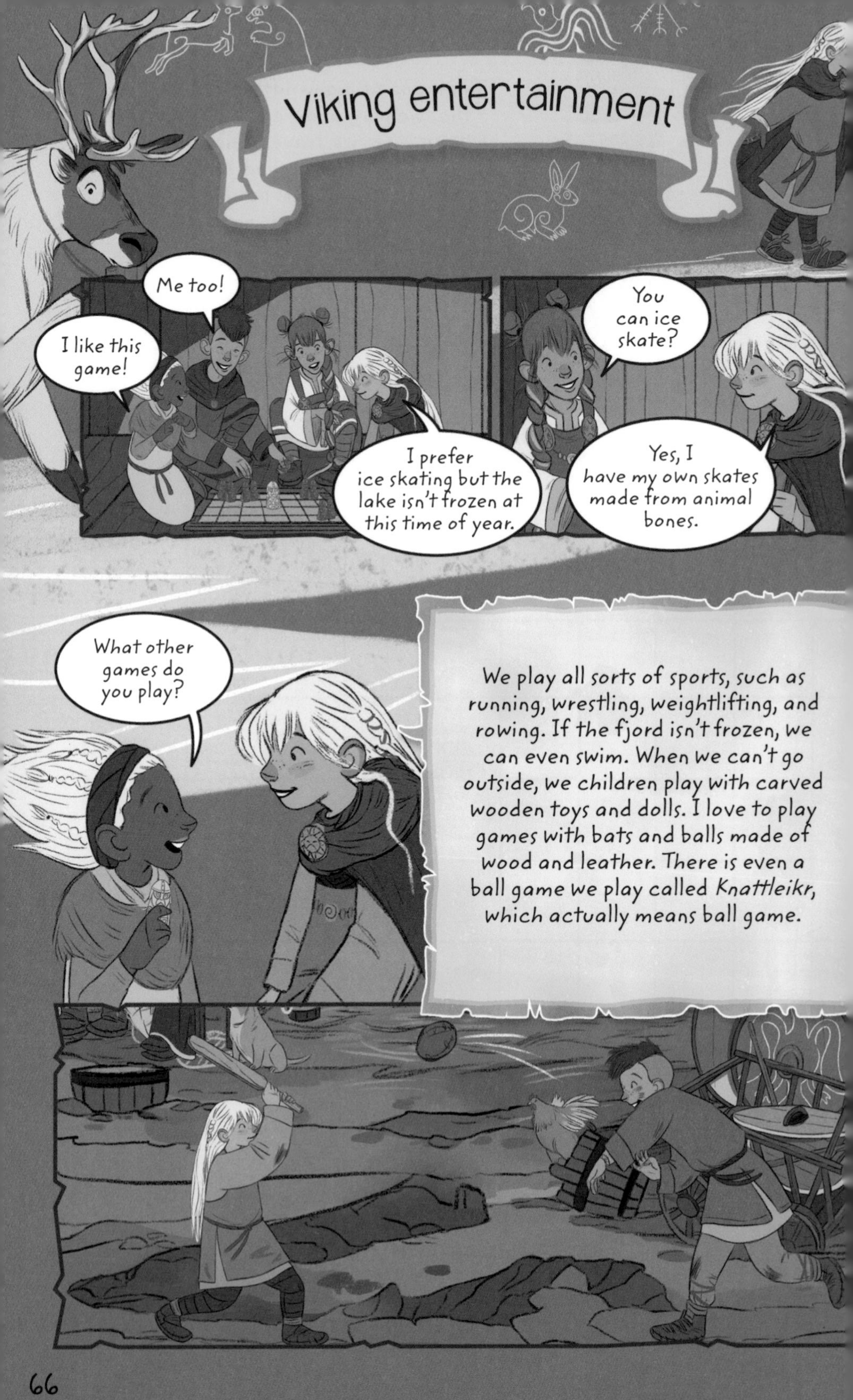

I like this game!
Me too!
I prefer ice skating but the lake isn't frozen at this time of year.
You can ice skate?
Yes, I have my own skates made from animal bones.
What other games do you play?
We play all sorts of sports, such as running, wrestling, weightlifting, and rowing. If the fjord isn't frozen, we can even swim. When we can't go outside, we children play with carved wooden toys and dolls. I love to play games with bats and balls made of wood and leather. There is even a ball game we play called *Knattleikr*, which actually means ball game.

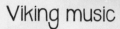

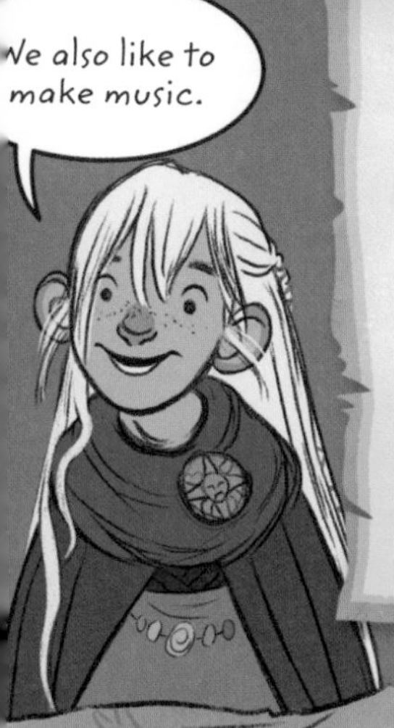
We also like to make music.

Viking music

- Archaeologists have found evidence of Viking musical instruments all over the lands in which they settled.
- They played flutes made from bones, panpipes made from wood, and rattles made from rings of iron.
- We also know from Viking stories that they played the harp and sang.
- Lots of examples of a simple instrument called a buzz bone or a bone spinner have also been found.

Write a song about the Vikings

Can you write a song about Viking adventures or the Norse gods?
It could describe the magnificent boats and the dangerous voyages. Or skies full of the brightest stars and strange new lands far from home.
Or the battles won by Thor with his hammer and the tricks played by Loki (turn the page for more information about these Norse gods).
What instrument would you play with your song? Would you bang a drum or play a harp?

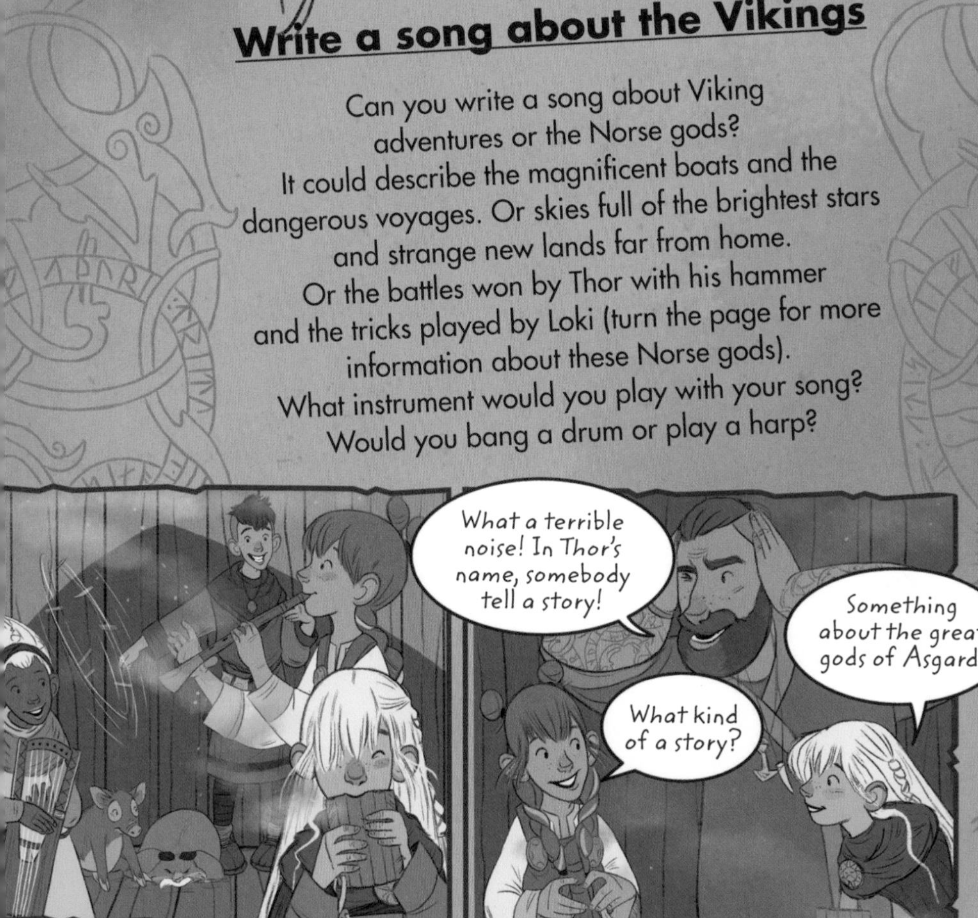
What a terrible noise! In Thor's name, somebody tell a story!
What kind of a story?
Something about the great gods of Asgard.

Gods and goddesses

Odin

Status: The god of war, wisdom, and death

Feature: Odin has only one eye, as he traded his other one for a drink from the Well of Wisdom.

"I am the ruler of the gods. I have a spear called Gugnir and I ride an eight-legged horse named Sleipnir."

Thor

Status: The god of thunder

Feature: Thor has red hair and a beard.

"I have a hammer called Mjolnir that I use to create thunder. When I throw it, it always returns to my hand."

Loki

Status: The god of trickery

Feature: Loki is a shape-shifter who can change his appearance.

"I am the father of many children, including a giant wolf, a serpent, and Odin's horse, Sleipnir."

Frigg

Status: The goddess of marriage and motherhood

Feature: Frigg can prophesy the future, but she never tells anyone what she knows.

"I am Odin's wife. Baldur is my son and Thor is my stepson. The day Friday is named after me."

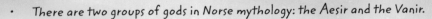

- There are two groups of gods in Norse mythology: the Aesir and the Vanir.
- The Aesir lived in Asgard.
- Vanaheim is the home of the Vanir.

Hel

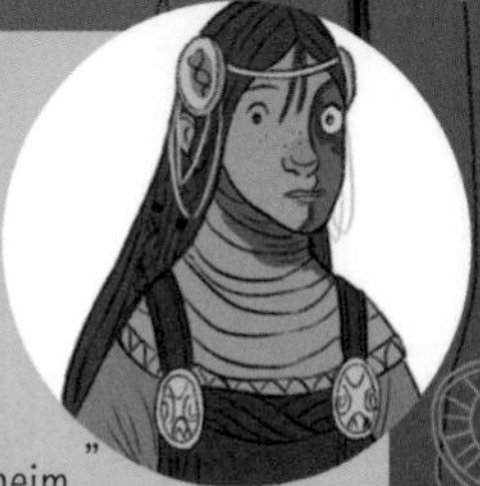

Status: The queen of the underworld

Feature: Half of Hel's face is dead and half of it is alive.

"I am the daughter of Loki and I look after those who have died and come to Helheim."

Freyja

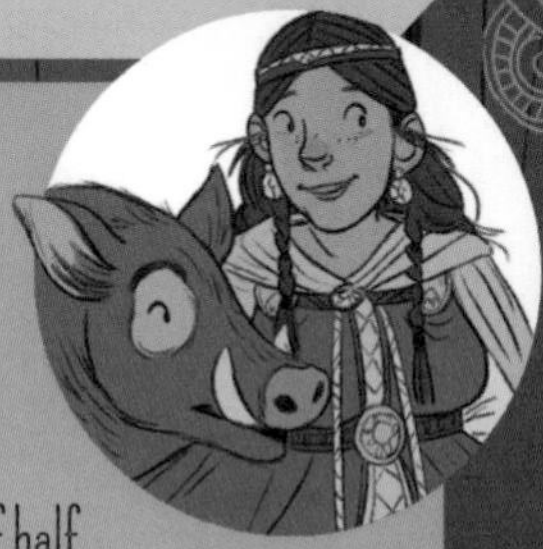

Status: The goddess of love and beauty

Feature: Freyja rides into battle on a golden boar named Hildisvíni.

"When I ride into battle alongside Viking warriors, I claim the souls of half of the slain heroes and take them to my field named Fólkvangr."

Baldur

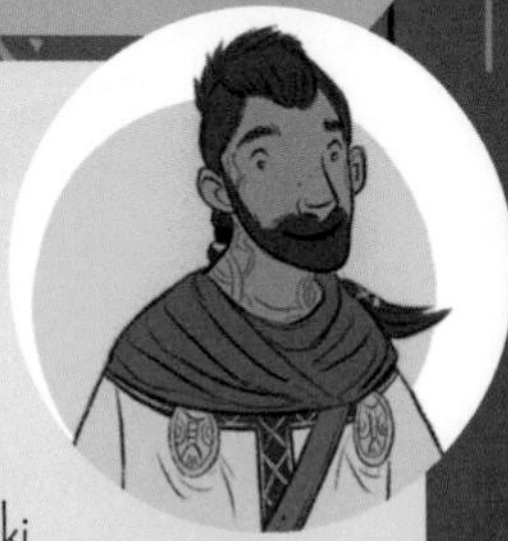

Status: The god of light, innocence, and peace

Feature: Baldur is so good and beautiful that light shines from him.

"I own *Hringhorni*, the greatest ship ever built. The mischievous god Loki tricked my blind brother Höðr into killing me."

Sif

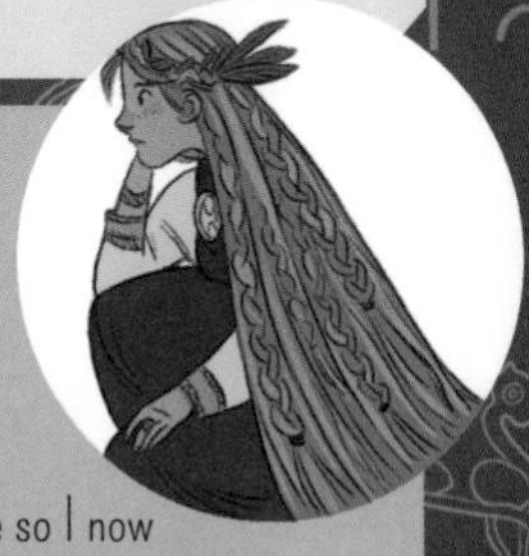

Status: The goddess of fertility

Feature: Sif's hair is made of gold.

"Loki cut off my hair. My husband, Thor, forced him to mend what he had done so I now have golden hair which was made by dwarf craftsmen."

Bragi

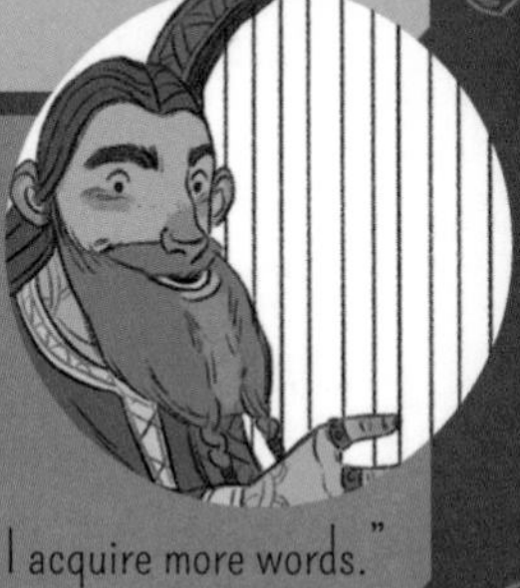

Status: The god of music, poetry, and storytelling

Feature: Bragi has a long beard and plays a harp.

am the storyteller of the gods and my wife, Iðunn, carves runes into my tongue so that I acquire more words."

Humans live in a world called Midgard, or Middle-Earth.

The nine worlds of Norse mythology were connected by the roots of a tree called Yggdrasil.

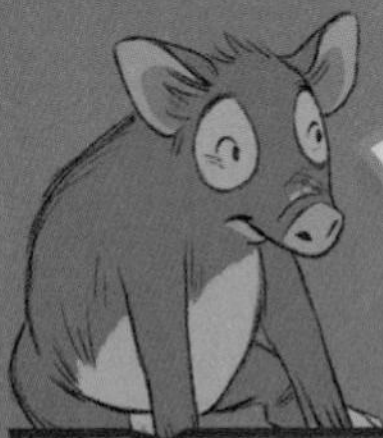

Norse stories

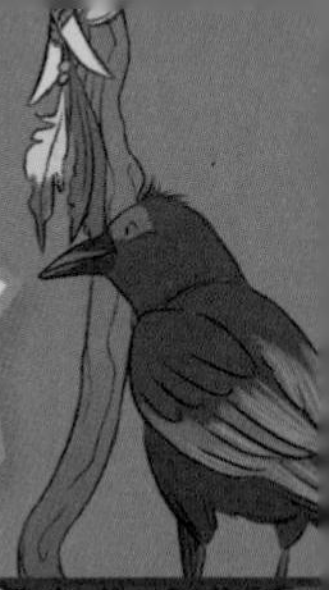

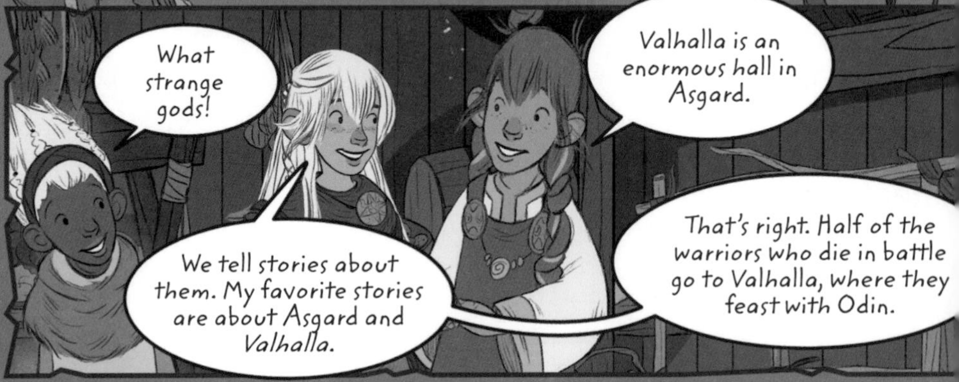
What strange gods!
We tell stories about them. My favorite stories are about Asgard and *Valhalla*.
Valhalla is an enormous hall in Asgard.
That's right. Half of the warriors who die in battle go to Valhalla, where they feast with Odin.

Telling stories

- The stories of the Norse gods were told by storytellers called **skalds**.
- These stories were not written down but were passed along orally.
- The skalds created and memorized these stories and would perform them for their Viking audiences.
- Only after the Norse people began to follow Christianity did writing become more common, and eventually these stories came to be written down and recorded.
- We call many of these stories **sagas**.

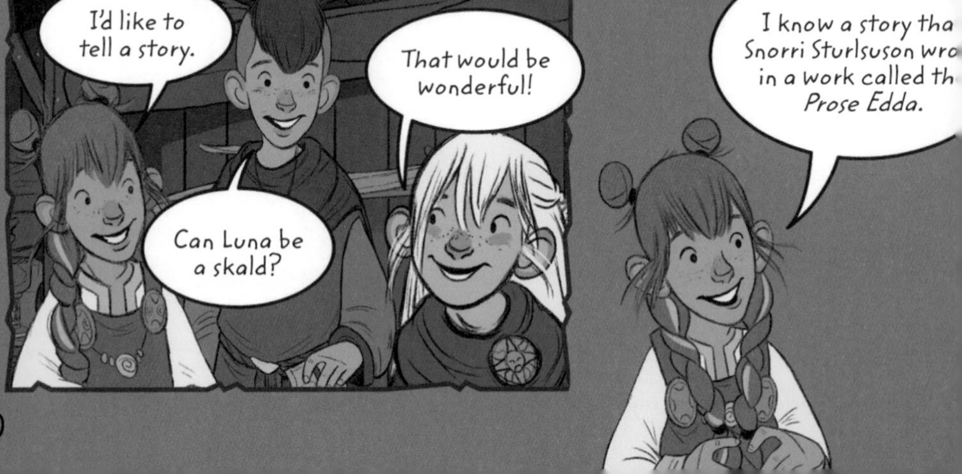
I'd like to tell a story.
Can Luna be a skald?
That would be wonderful!
I know a story tha
Snorri Sturlsuson wro
in a work called th
Prose Edda.

Read this story aloud.

Before the world existed, there was an enormous abyss
called Ginnungagap. On either side of the abyss lay
Muspelheim, the land of fire, and Niflheim, the land of ice.
The frost and the flames from these two lands met in
Ginnungagap, where they formed the giant named Ymir.
He was the father to all of the giants because from his
sweat, his children were born.
Out of the melting ice emerged the gods of the Aesir tribe.
The gods and giants lived side by side and eventually the god
Bor and the giant Bestla had three sons who they
named Odin, Vili, and Ve.
One day, Ymir became evil, so these three brothers
killed him and they used his body to create the world.
They used his flesh and bones to build the land and
the mountains. They made rivers and oceans out of his blood.
His teeth became rocks and boulders, and his brain became
the clouds. They positioned Ymir's skullcap over the
earth to make the sky, and it was held up by four dwarves
who marked out north, south, east, and west.
The brothers took two tree trunks and turned them into
Ask and Embla, the very first man and woman.
The sparks of fire that came from Muspelheim became
the Sun, the Moon, and the stars, which lit the world.
The Sun and the Moon are pulled across the sky by chariots,
which are chased by enormous wolf giants named
Skoll and Hati.
The gods connected the land of men with their own
home, Asgard, by a rainbow bridge called Bifrost.
When they had finished their work, the gods named the
world they created Midgard, or Middle-Earth, and they used
Ymir's eyelashes to form a wall around the earth, which
would keep the giants out.

The feast

Feasting

- The Vikings ate regular feasts throughout the year.

- They celebrated three main festivals: one at the beginning of winter, called **Vetrnætr**, one in midwinter, called **Jól**, and one at the beginning of summer, known as **Sumarmál**.

- Other feasts were held to celebrate good harvests, successful raids, and funerals.

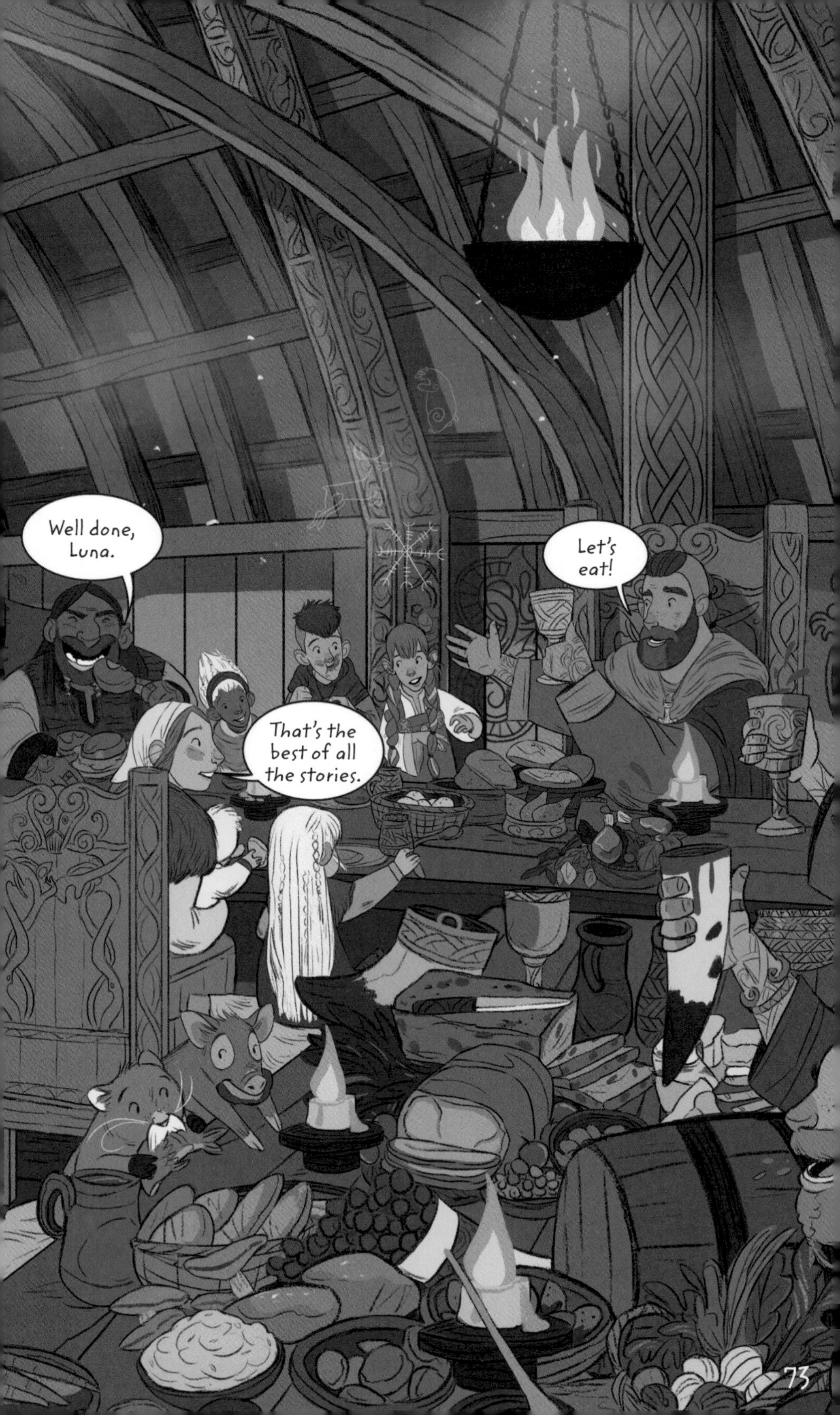
Well done, Luna.
Let's eat!
That's the best of all the stories.

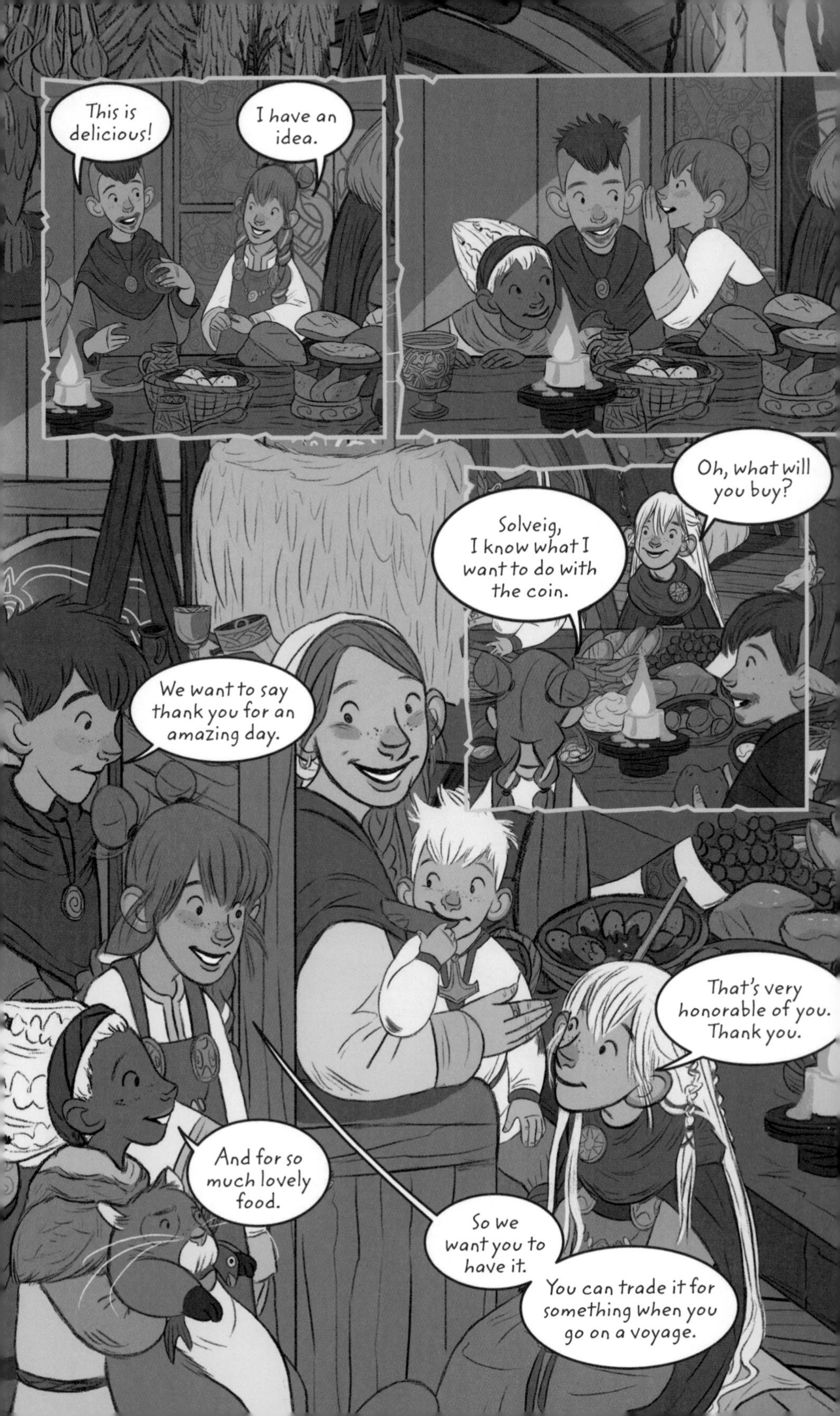
This is delicious!
I have an idea.
Oh, what will you buy?
Solveig, I know what I want to do with the coin.
We want to say thank you for an amazing day.
That's very honorable of you. Thank you.
And for so much lovely food.
So we want you to have it.
You can trade it for something when you go on a voyage.

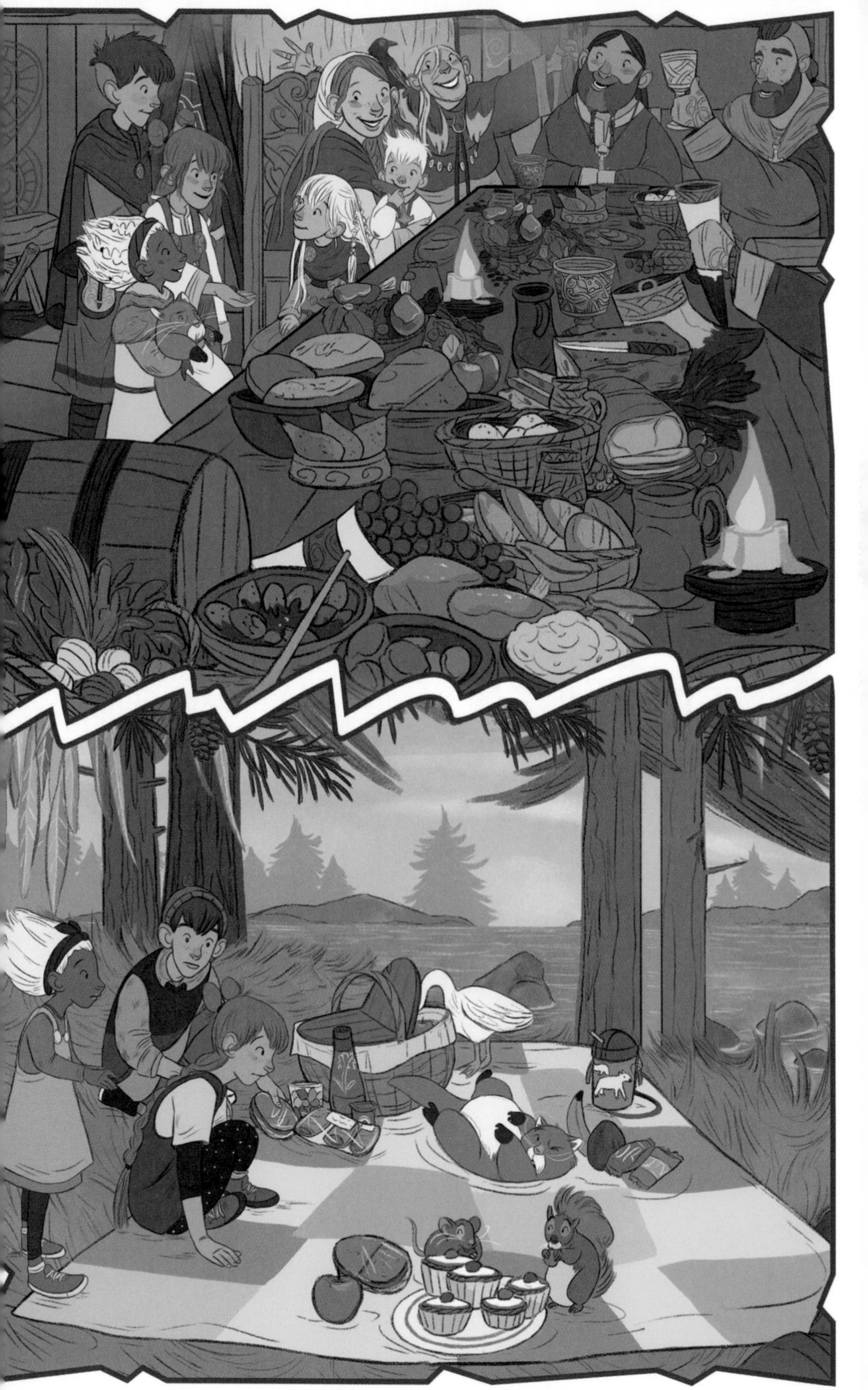

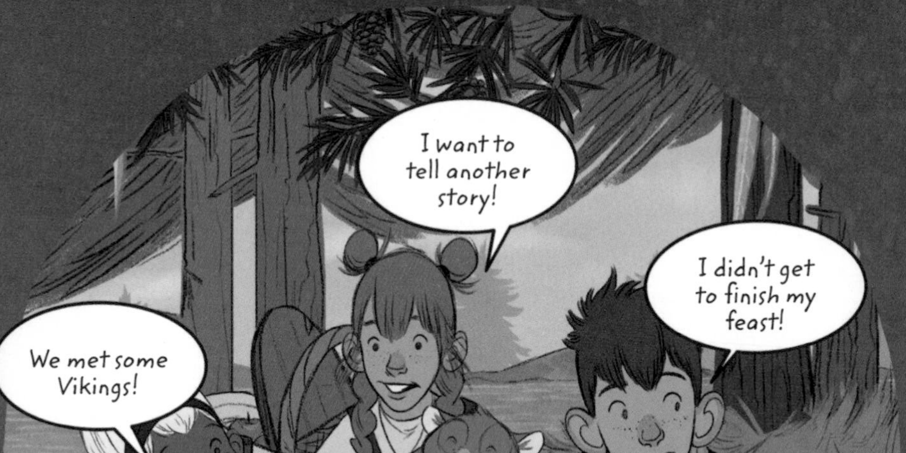
We met some Vikings!
I want to tell another story!
I didn't get to finish my feast!

Quiz questions

1. Who is the Viking god of thunder?

   a) Thor
   b) Zeus
   c) Hermes

2. What is a Viking "thing"?

   a) A party
   b) A law-making assembly
   c) A school

3. What is mead made from?

   a) Honey
   b) Spinach
   c) Cheese

4. With which symbols did the Vikings write?

   a) Hieroglyphs
   b) Runes
   c) Ticks

5. What is the name of the star the Vikings used to find north?

   a) Vega
   b) Betelgeuse
   c) Leiðarstjarna

6. What is the name for broken pieces of silver used for trade?

   a) Hacksilver
   b) Brokesilver
   c) Piecesilver

7. What is the name for a Viking storyteller?

   a) Bard
   b) Minstrel
   c) Skald

8. Which special Viking weapons were given names?

   a) Axes
   b) Arrows
   c) Swords

9. What is the name for a Viking warship?

   a) Longship
   b) Narrow boat
   c) Yacht

10. What is Asgard?

   a) A boy's name
   b) The home of the gods
   c) A type of fish

Answers

pp. 34–35

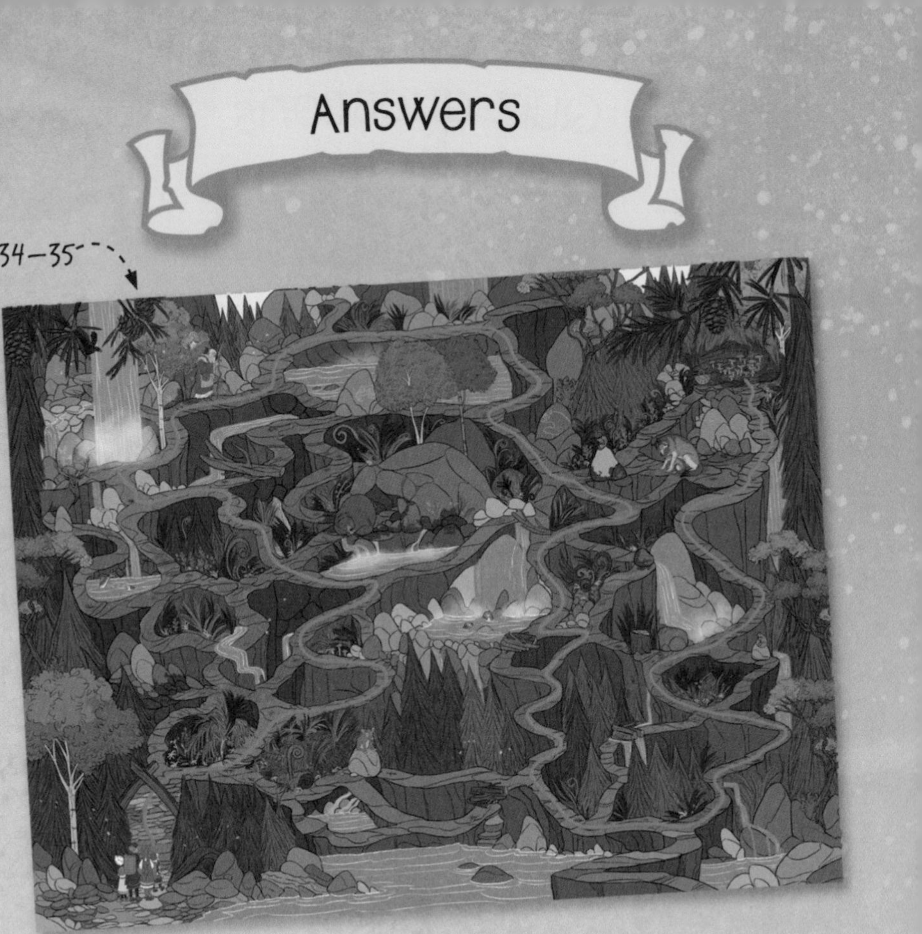

pp. 38–39

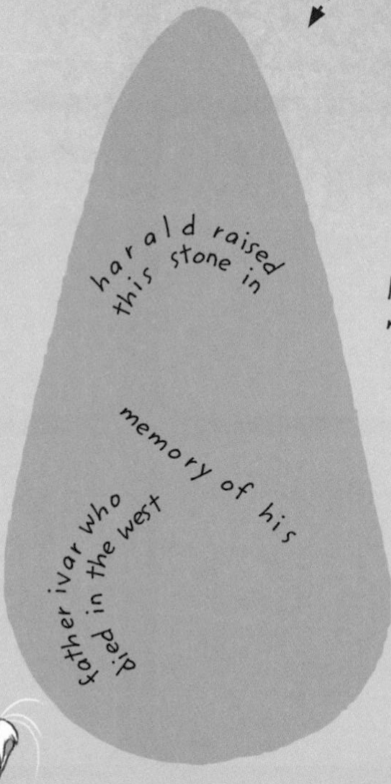
harald raised this stone in
memory of his
father ivar who died in the west

Harald raised this stone in memory of his father Ivar who died in the west.

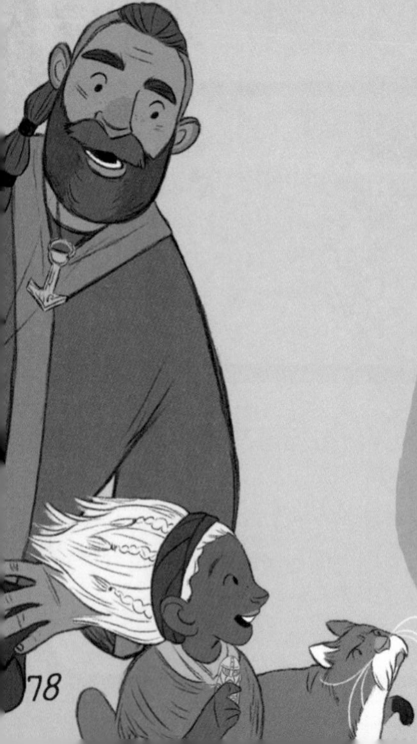

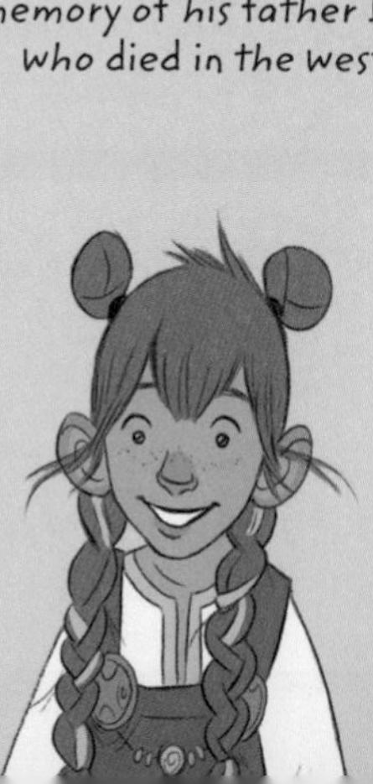

pp. 42—43

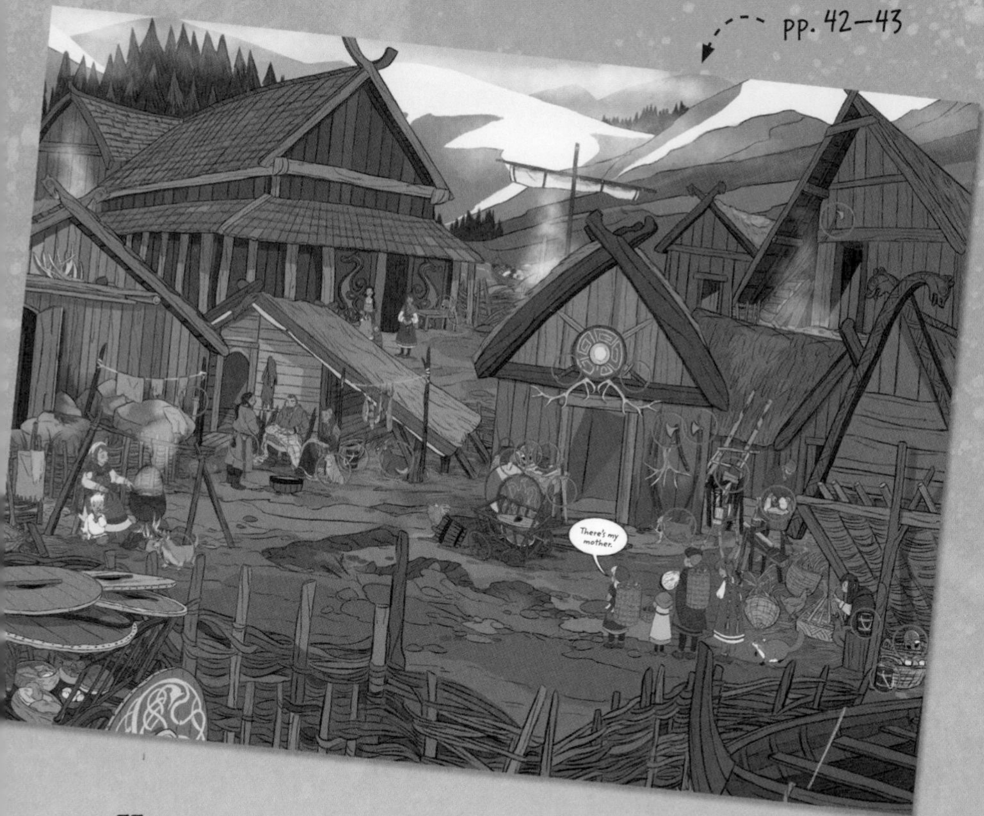
There's my mother.

p. 77

1. a 2. b
3. a 4. b
5. c 6. a
7. c 8. c
9. a 10. b

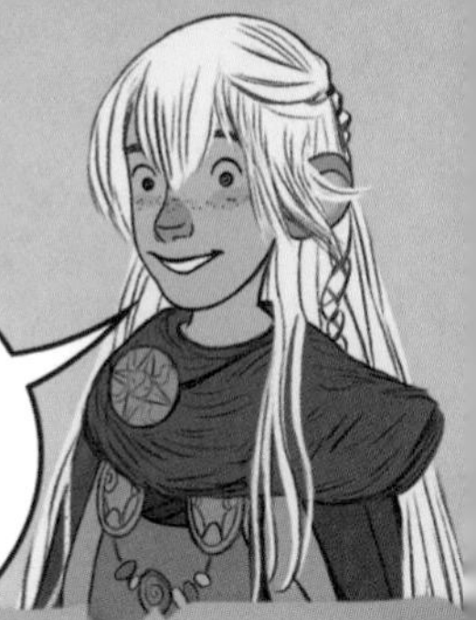

When we write Old Norse in a modern alphabet, it contains some letters that you might not recognize. Can you find these letters?

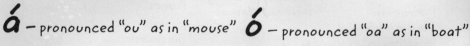

á – pronounced "ou" as in "mouse"

í – pronounced "ee" as in "feet"

ð – pronounced "th" as in "that"

ö – pronounced "u" as in "burn"

ó – pronounced "oa" as in "boat"

ú – pronounced "oo" as in "zoo"

æ – pronounced "i" as in "ice"

GLOSSARY

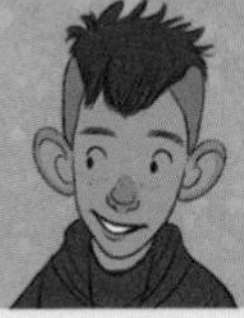

Aurar
(oy-rar)
A measure of weight

Dagverðr
(dag-ver-thur)
The name for a meal eaten in the morning

Daub
(dawb)
A mixture of mud, straw, and manure for covering the walls of houses

Dönsk tunga
(dunsk tung-a)
The language spoken by the Vikings

Eyrir
(ey-reer)
A measure that is roughly 1 ounce (28g) in weight

Forage
(forr-ij)
To search for food that grows in the wild

Hafvilla
(haf-vit-la)
The Old Norse word for getting lost at sea

Hnefatafl
(ne-fa-ta-full)
A type of board game

Jarl
(yarl)
A Viking nobleman

Jól
(yole)
A feast that took place in mid-January

Karl
(carl)
A Viking freeman

Keel
(key-l)
The beam that makes the base of a boat

Langhús
(lang-hoos)
A longhouse in which the Vikings lived

Leiðarstjarna
(lay-tha-stee-ar-na)
The Viking name for the North Star

Loom
(loom)
A frame for weaving thread into fabric

Mast
(maast)
A post in the center of a boat from which a sail is suspended

Mörk
(merk)
A measure that weighs the same as 8 aurar. The plural of mörk is merker.

Nalbinding
(narl-bine-ding)
A technique for turning thread into fabric

Náttverðr
(nowt-ver-thur)
The name for a meal eaten at nighttime

Naust
(noyst)
A boathouse

Örtug
(er-tug)
A measure that is roughly 1/3 of an eyrir

Pund
(pund)
A measure worth 24 merkur

Runes
(roonz)
The symbols that made up the alphabet of northern Europe up until the thirteenth century

Saga
(sah-ga)
A legendary story about heroic event

Skald
(skald)
A Viking storytelle

Stern
(sturn)
The back of a boat

Sumarmál
(sum-ar-mawl)
A feast that took place in mid-April

Thrall
(thrawl)
A Viking slave

Vetrnætr
(vet-ur-nigh-tur)
A feast that took place in mid-October

Víka sjóvar
(vee-ka see-oh-va
The distance traveled by around 1,000 rowing strok

Wattle
(wot-tuhl)
A woven wooden framework for making the walls of houses

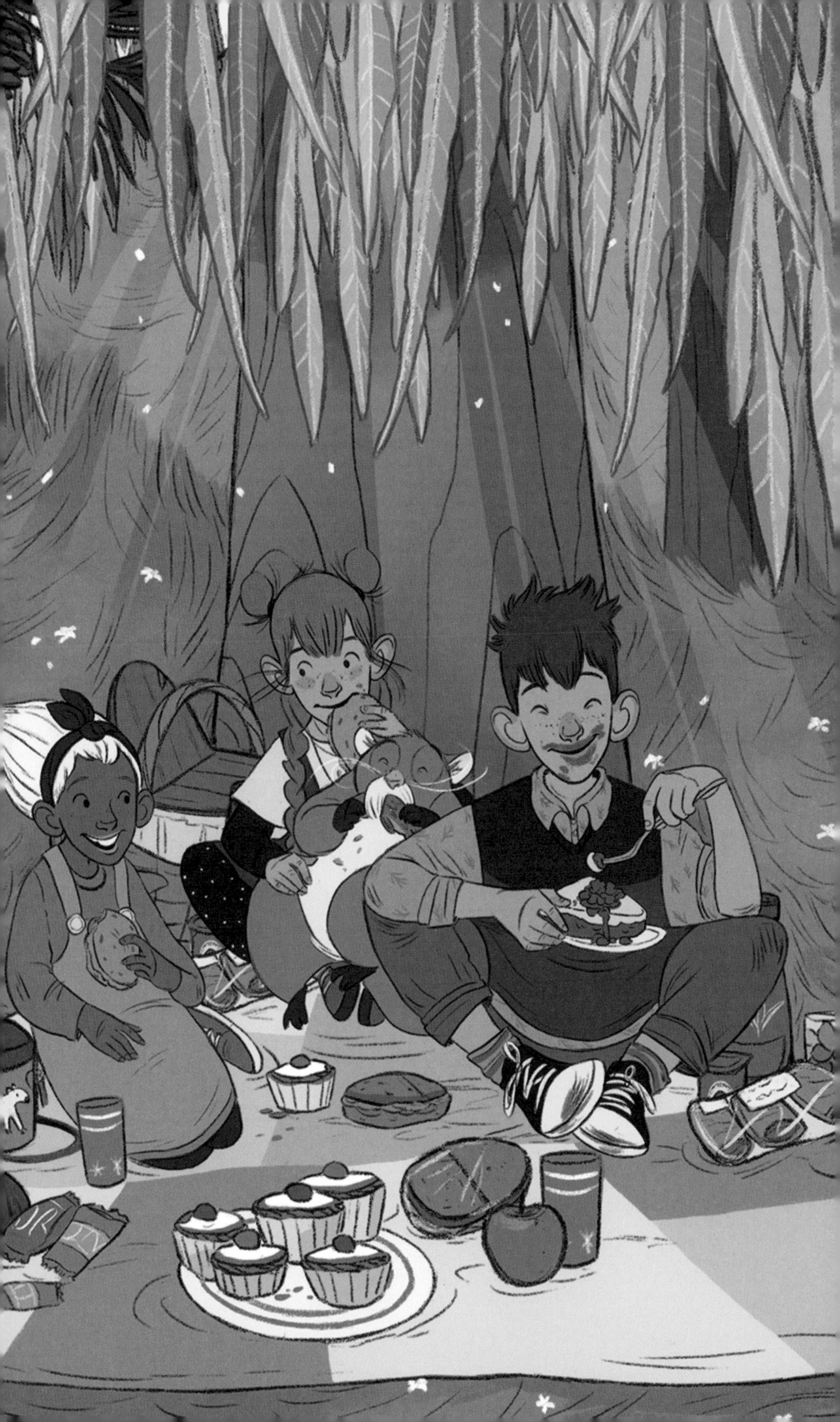

About the author and illustrator

Spot the author and illustrator in the book!

Frances is a historian and dedicated castle visitor. She can usually be found in the library surrounded by stacks of books that she can't wait to read.
Likes: Books, holidays, thunder storms, trains, and the theater
Dislikes: Washing up
Favorite Color: Purple
Favorite Food: Fish and chips
Favorite Places: Libraries and castles

Grace is an illustrator and animator. She loves to explore with her two dogs, Muffin and Kodie-bear.
Likes: Adventures, the ocean, fairy lights, olives, and animals
Dislikes: Having wet socks
Favorite Color: Turquoise
Favorite Food: Apple crumble
Favorite Places: Forests and outer space

Ready for more adventures with The Histronauts?
Here's a sneak peek of *A Roman Adventure!*

·THE·
HISTRONAUTS

A ROMAN ADVENTURE

Written by
FRANCES DURKIN

Illustrated by
GRACE COOKE

Designed by
VICKY BARKER

JOLLY FISH PRESS

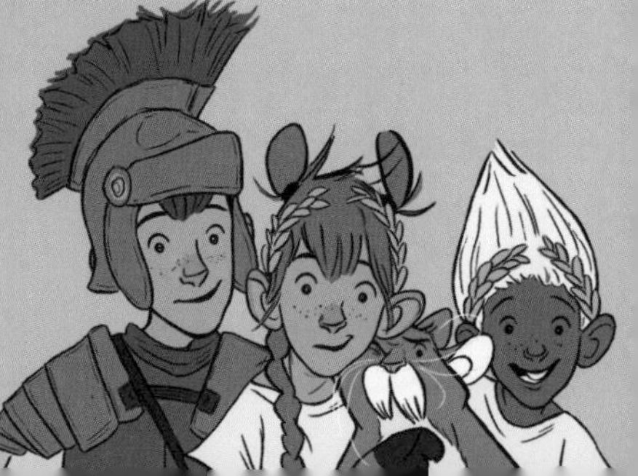

A new friend from a different time

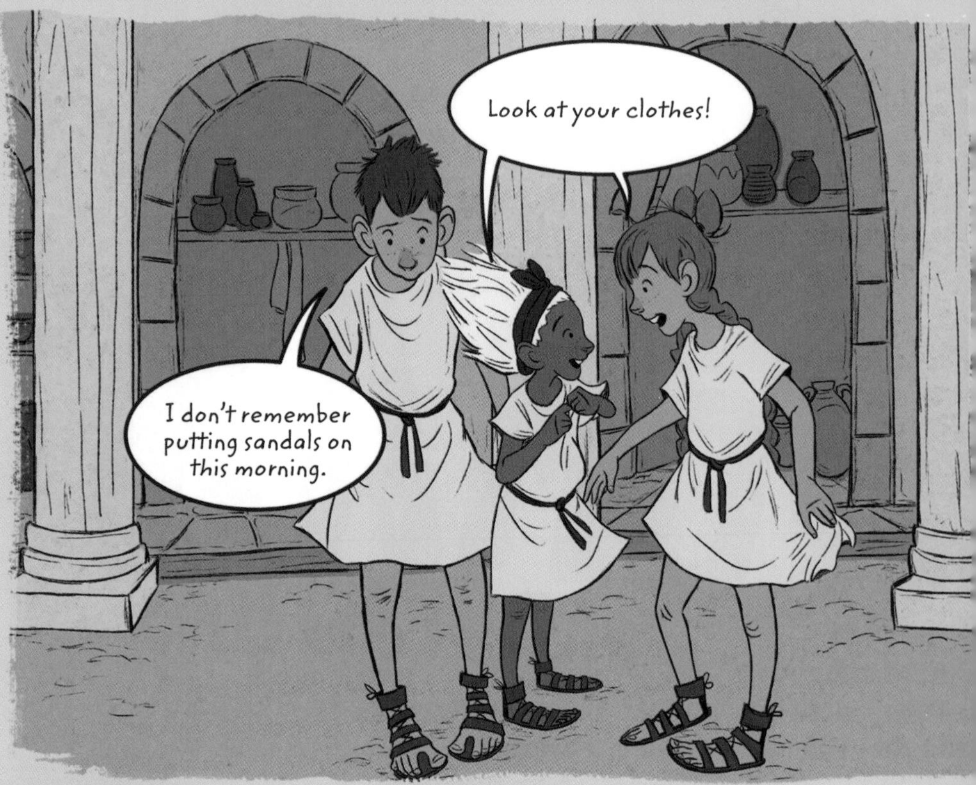
Look at your clothes!
I don't remember putting sandals on this morning.

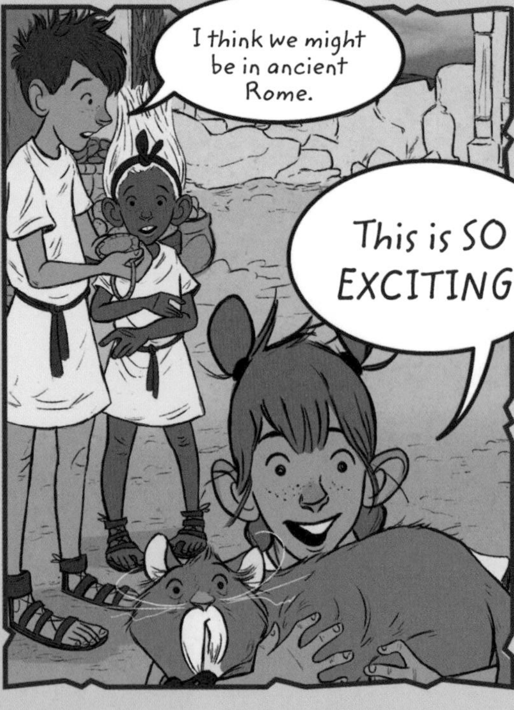
I think we might be in ancient Rome.
This is SO EXCITING!

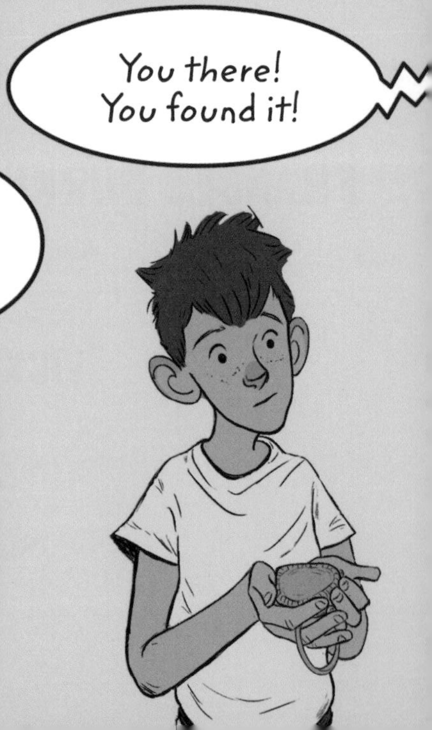
You there! You found it!

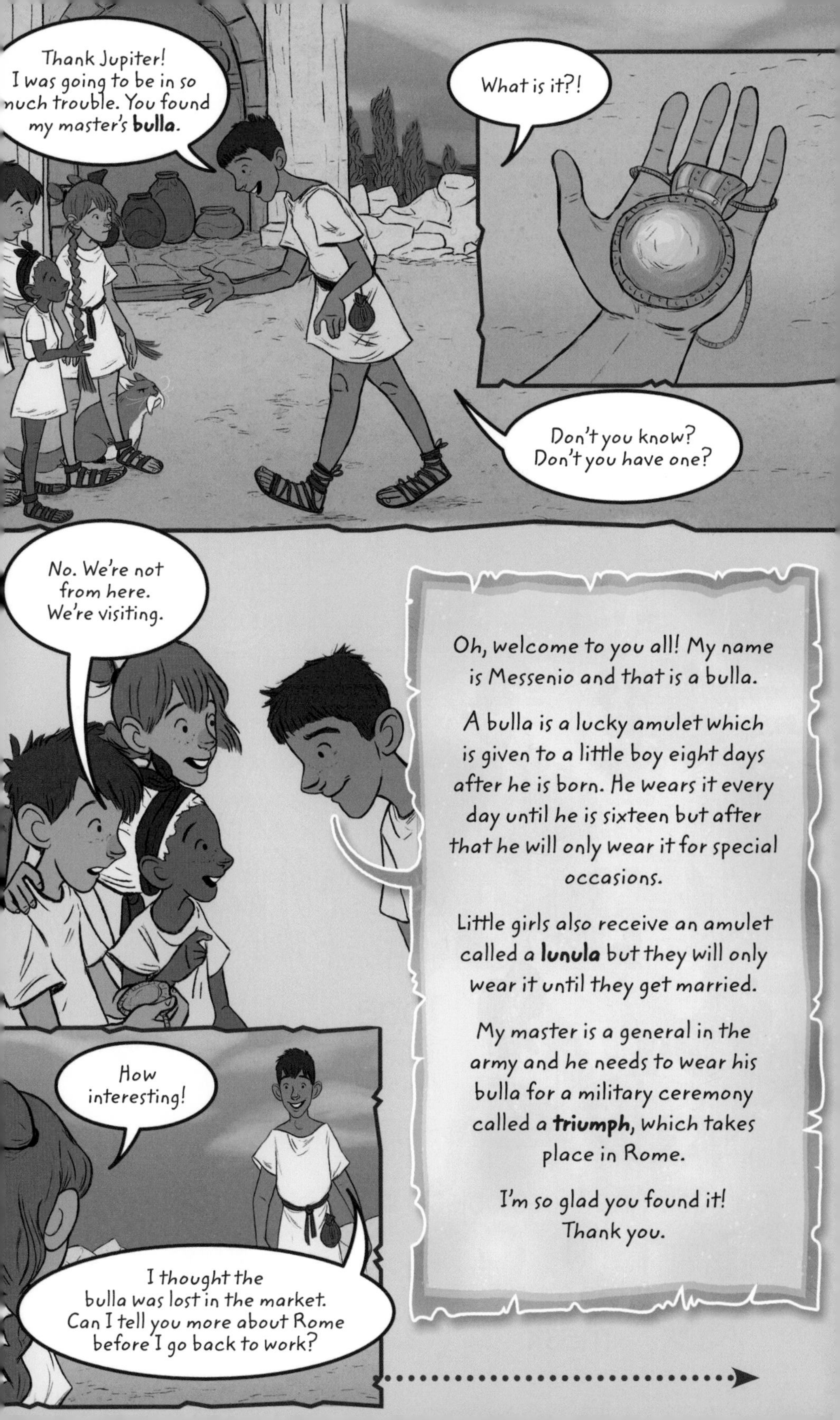
Thank Jupiter! I was going to be in so much trouble. You found my master's **bulla**.
What is it?!
Don't you know? Don't you have one?
No. We're not from here. We're visiting.
Oh, welcome to you all! My name is Messenio and that is a bulla.
A bulla is a lucky amulet which is given to a little boy eight days after he is born. He wears it every day until he is sixteen but after that he will only wear it for special occasions.
Little girls also receive an amulet called a **lunula** but they will only wear it until they get married.
My master is a general in the army and he needs to wear his bulla for a military ceremony called a **triumph**, which takes place in Rome.
I'm so glad you found it! Thank you.
How interesting!
I thought the bulla was lost in the market. Can I tell you more about Rome before I go back to work?

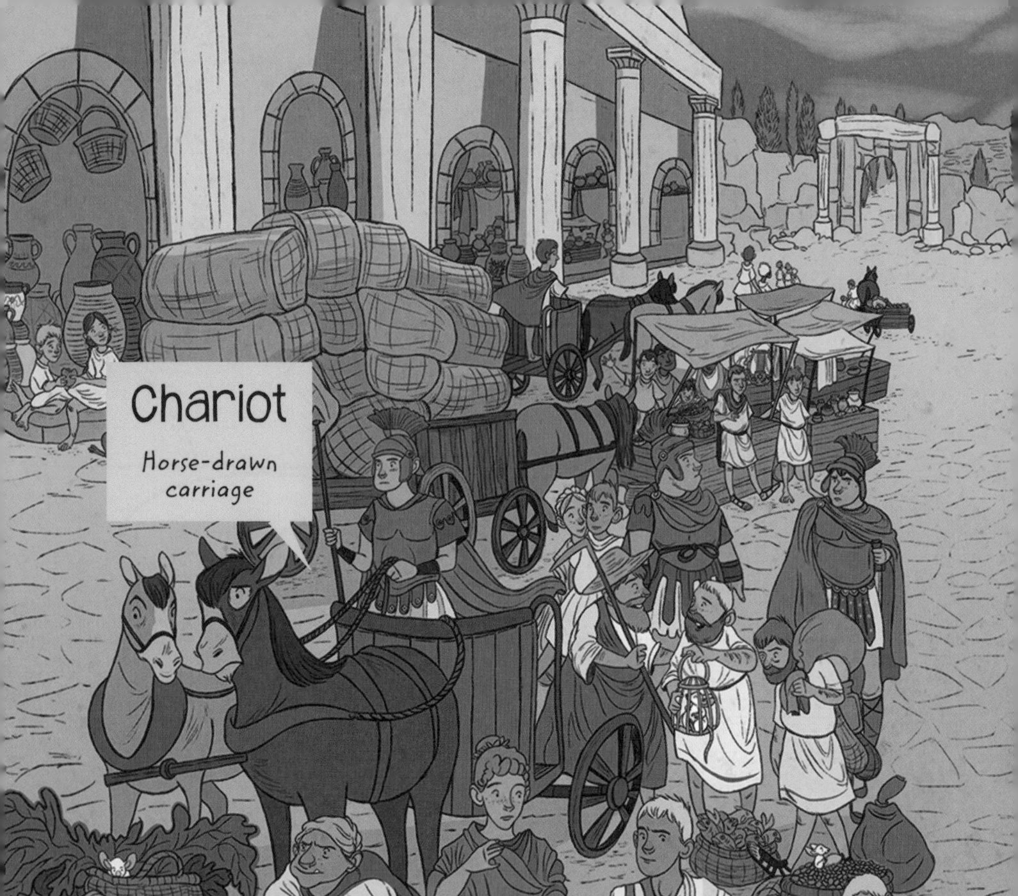
Chariot
Horse-drawn carriage
Toga
Worn by rich men

Can you find these objects in the busy market scene?

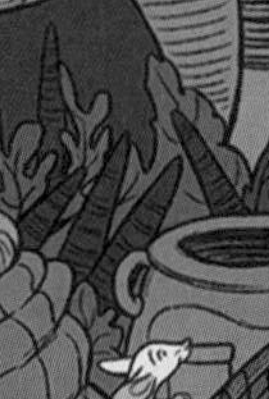

1 theater mask

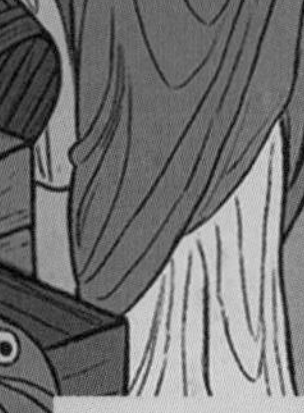

7 mice

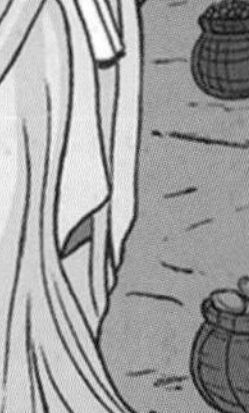

2 lyres

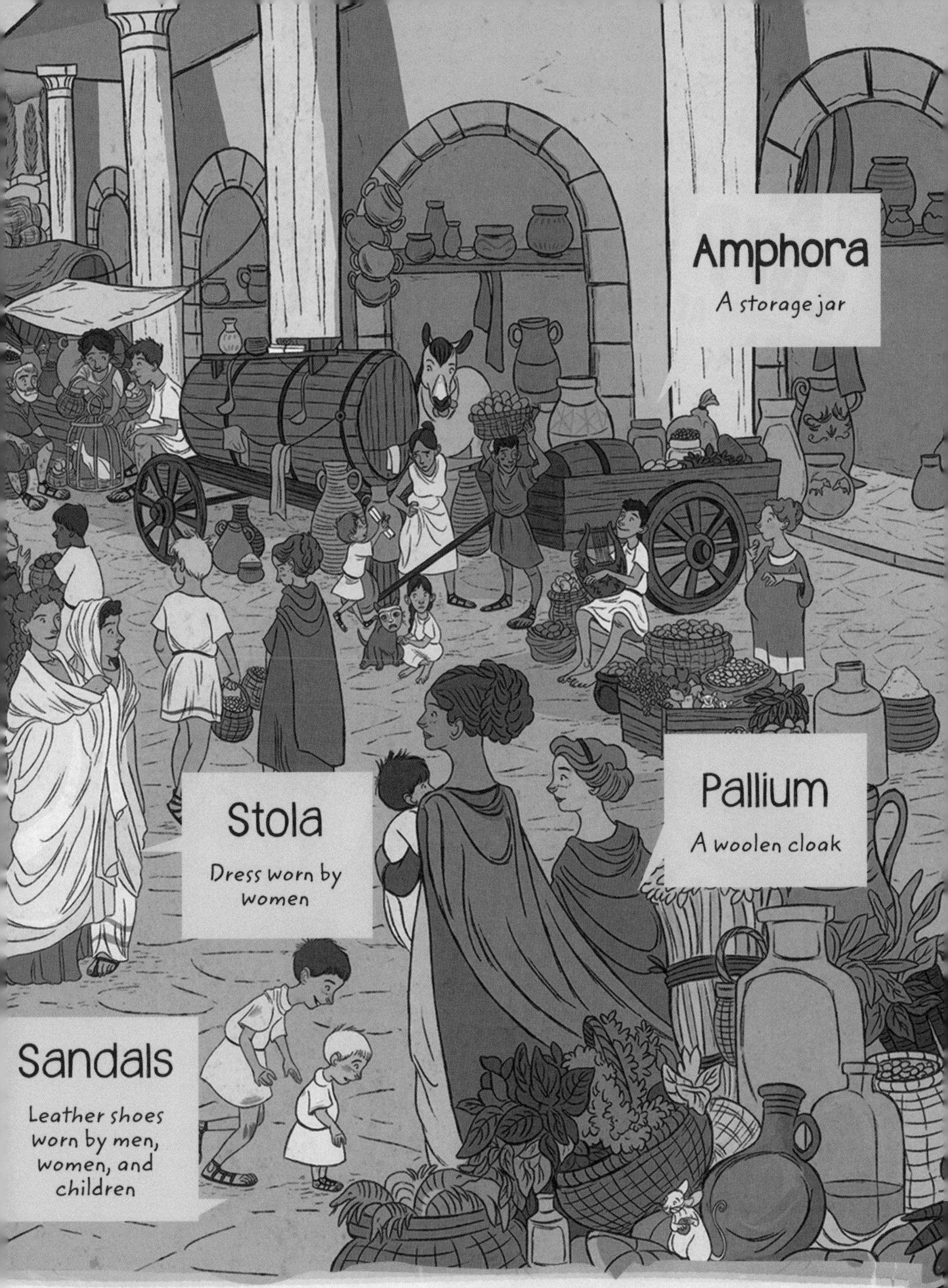
Amphora
A storage jar
Stola
Dress worn by women
Pallium
A woolen cloak
Sandals
Leather shoes worn by men, women, and children

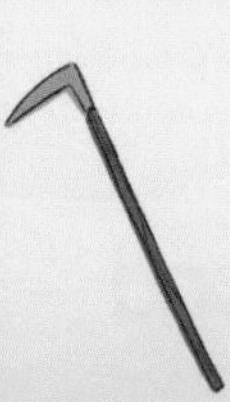
1 farm tool

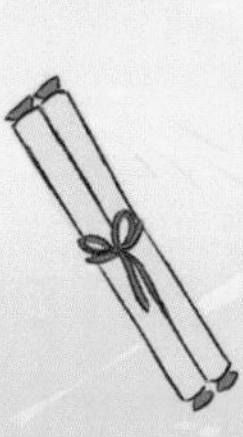
3 scrolls

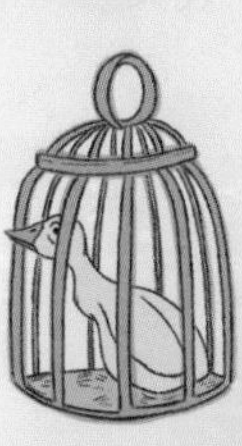
1 bird in a cage

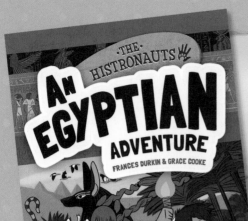